Cliff's Edge

Willow Springs Ranch
Laura Harner

Cliff's Edge is a work of fiction. Names, characters, places, and incidents are the product of the author's imagination or are used fictitiously. Any resemblance to actual persons, living or dead, events, or locales is entirely coincidental.

Contents

Dedication

When I first wrote Ty Hard, Willow Springs Ranch Book 1, I had no real idea of how much the readers would fall in love with my guys. This series really signaled a new beginning in my writing life. Here we are 6.5 books later, and Cliff and Ryan are ushering another new beginning. I hope you love them every bit as much as Ty and Cass.

Thank you to my writing partners: Havan Fellows, Lee Brazil, Will Parkinson, and Tom Webb—I love spending every day in Google chat writing with you.

A very special thank you to Mardee Barnett, Christy Duke, Mary Wallace, and as always, Jae Ashley.

Finally, I would like to thank you, my wonderful reader. I couldn't have done this without each and every one of you. Thank you, for all your support.

Trademark Acknowledgements

The author acknowledges the trademarked status and trademark owners of the following trademarks mentioned in this work of fiction:

Big Red: WM. Wrigley Jr. Company

Coke: The Coca-Cola Company

Corona: Cerveceria Modelo, S.A. de C.V.

Day-Glo: Day-Glo Color Corp.

Dirty Jobs: Discovery Communications, LLC

Gator (4-wheeler): Deere & Company

Google: Google, Inc.

Guinness: Diageo Ireland

iPhone: Apple, Inc.

iPod: Apple, Inc.

Jack (referencing Jack Daniel beverage): Jack Daniel's Properties, Inc.

Jeep: Chrysler Group, LLC

Keurig: Keurig, Inc.

Luminox: Lumondi, Inc.

NCIS: CBS Studios Inc.

Netflix: Netflix, Inc.

New England Patriots: New England Patriots LLC

San Diego Chargers: Chargers Football Company, LLC

San Diego Padres: Padres L.P. Padres, Inc.

SEALs: The Department of the Navy

Seattle Seahawks: Football Northwest LLC

SIG 226 & SIG: SIG Swiss Industrial Company

Skilcraft (clock): National Industries for the Blind

Sons of Anarchy: Twentieth Century Fox Film Corporation

So You Think You Can Dance: Dick Clark Productions, Inc.

SpongeBob SquarePants: Viacom International Inc.

US Army: Department of the Army

Wranglers: Wrangler Apparel Corp.

.

Chapter One

"Black and tan. I'll watch while you pull," Cliff told the bow-tied, bare-chested bartender.

"Very good, Sir. I always enjoy being watched while I'm pulling," the cheeky man behind the bar replied with a smile.

Laughing, Cliff dragged a high-backed stool closer as he looked beyond the taps to survey the Thursday night crowd. Although he'd only been to the club half a dozen times in as many years, the interior was as he'd remembered. Dark wood wainscoting, white with red fleur-de-lis accented wallpaper, and swathes of heavy red fabric draped around the room, masking the interior-sealed windows. Elaborate gold and crystal chandeliers glowed softly over the burgundy leather tufted-back sofas, chaise lounges, ornate side chairs, and decor tables. If the cavernous room had been devoid of people and props, you could almost believe you'd stepped into a long ago Victorian parlor. Cliff snorted. Okay, maybe a Victorian brothel. His gaze settled on the woman clad only in a black silk bustier, bound face-first against the St. Andrews cross.

Behind her, a man wielded a flogger, drawing up a shade of pink across her ass and thighs.

Mostly ignoring the scene in the center of the room, men and women stood talking or sat in one of the many conversational groupings, some actively engaged in play, others watched, and a few people drifted from spot to spot, seemingly entranced by their surroundings.

Turning to study the others who'd elected to sit at the bar, Cliff noticed most of them were men, dressed in business casual. Some of the drinkers might be starting a long weekend and didn't have to be to work until Monday, but Cliff would bet more than a few would have serious regrets when they hit the desk tomorrow morning. Several pretended an interest in the bottom of their glasses, but most followed the bartender's slim hips as he worked the crowded bar. The glass of Guinness sat nearly full to the side of the beer taps while the pretty dark-haired man stepped to the opposite end of the bar to pour a Jack and Coke for another customer. He moved with a slightly exaggerated graceful efficiency that said he was aware of the admiring glances. By the time he returned to Cliff's end of the long bar, the dark brew had settled. He added the last inch, holding the glass straight up so the head rounded perfectly above the rim. So many suggestive comments played in Cliff's head, but in the end, he settled for a quick thanks as the bartender placed the perfectly stacked Guinness on a circular coaster.

"Running a tab tonight, Sir?"

Cliff tossed a bill on the bar. "No thanks—this is it for me," he said, raising the glass in toast. He tilted it just enough to take a mouthful of foam along with the velvet smooth brew nearly thick enough to make a meal. "Mmmm...perfect. Keep the change."

The slender young man's brows rose at the generous tip. "Thank you. My name's Gentry. I don't think I've seen you around Hard Labour before, Sir..." He vigorously swiped at a nonexistent stain on the gleaming oak while he waited to see if Cliff would take the conversational bait.

"Oh, I've been here a few times," Cliff assured him. He licked the foam from his lips, enjoying the way the big, blue eyes followed every movement of his tongue. He raised a brow. "Is Draco around?"

"Oh—" Gentry's gaze darted to the dimly lit staircase that ran along the wall. "May I tell him who's asking?"

"Cliff. A friend of Rhino's. Draco's expecting me." Damn...he wished Rhino was in CONUS. He should have talked to his best friend first.

"Sure...I'll call and let him know you're here." He swished his narrow hips a little as he walked to the register, rang up the drink, and dropped the change in a tip jar. He tossed a quick wink over his shoulder, then turned away to use the phone hanging on the wall.

Five minutes later, Gentry stepped around the bar and ushered Cliff to the bottom of the stairs. "Just call out if there's anything at all I can do for you, Sir. Oh, and you forgot this." He shoved the coaster into Cliff's hand. Looking down, he saw the man's name scrawled across the back, along with a phone number.

"Thanks, Gentry. I'll keep that in mind."

Taking the steps two at a time, Cliff Snyder bounded up the half staircase leading to the loft that served as the office for the club manager. Now that he made up his mind—sort of—he was anxious to get on with the mission. He gave himself a mental snort. Okay, so maybe looking into club membership and training as a Dom wasn't exactly the same thing as the life or death assignments that were part of his job. Given his teammates often referred to him as Cool Hand when he was deep in demolition mode, anyone he worked with would be laughing at his current case of uncertainty.

He tapped on the door and entered at the shouted, "Come in."

The man striding toward him was striking. With his square face creased into a broad smile, he reminded Cliff of Harrison Ford in a craggy kind of way. "Cliff, nice to see you again," he said, hand extended.

Accepting both the handshake and the polite lie, Cliff followed the club owner inside. Draco Kincaid would have no reason to remember meeting him more than two years earlier.

"Thanks for seeing me. I have— Shit. What the hell do I have?" He laughed and shook his head.

"A few questions?" Draco supplied. "Come on. Let's have a seat and talk." The room was divided into two distinct areas. Directly in front of them and lining the left wall was the office space. In addition to a traditionally styled oak desk with a rolling leather chair, there were filing cabinets, a small safe, and a metal equipment rack with shelves holding miniature security monitors. In the center, a twenty-seven inch display cycled through each camera view, the image hovering on the screen for less than ten seconds before shifting to the next. It was a dizzying array of club scenes and private sessions, but before the screen changed views three times, Draco pressed a button on a small remote, and the monitors went dark. "The cameras are monitored from another room," Draco said by way of explanation as they passed through the open office to the sitting area along the far wall.

"This is my own private space…no cameras. I have the office and this sitting area…" He pressed another button on the remote and a small whir sounded from the bookshelf that lined the opposite wall. The shelves divided down the center, rolling away to reveal another room, shrouded in darkness. With a dramatic flourish and a wicked grin, Draco pushed the remote once more, and lights in the secret room flickered like a dozen candles had been lit.

Cliff laughed. "Just what every man needs…a bed in his office. I suppose it's your version of a casting couch—oh, shit. That sounded wrong."

"No offense taken," Draco said with a little chuckle. "Sometimes that's exactly what it is. When I hire staff members for certain positions, I need to test the limits of their control. Besides, someone's gotta test the toys before we equip the private rooms."

"Too bad *Dirty Jobs* went off the air—that would be an episode to remember."

"Speaking of remembering—I do, you know. You came here with Rhino two years ago. And you'd been here with him three or four times before that." Draco frowned. "I'm surprised you didn't bring him along if you have questions about the lifestyle. Most couples usually come together. So to speak."

"Me and Rhino?" Cliff shook his head. "We play for different teams."

"Ahh…yes. I have seen him here a time or two with different women. My mistake." Draco stared at him until Cliff wanted to rub his face to check for dirt.

"Do I…do I *know* you? Beyond those meetings, I mean?"

Draco smiled. "No, as I said, I remember you...but maybe it's more important that I *know* about you. Or at least I know why you might enjoy some of the entertainment options available at Hard Labour..." Reaching into his pocket, Draco withdrew something small enough to hide in his hand. He held it tightly for a long moment. "I asked Rhino never to mention how we met—it was only briefly and before I opened this club." He side-armed the item across to Cliff, who snatched it then stared, a smile hovering over his lips.

"Well, I'll be a sonofabitch," he said as he stared at the gold trident. Draco Kincaid had been a Navy SEAL.

"It's why I agreed to answer your questions rather than have you attend a couple of our introductory meetings. BDSM is different for people like us."

"Like us? Because of our training?"

"Exactly. Tell me. What part of BDSM have you tried? Or is it all just fantasy to you at this point? Sorry to be so blunt, but you wanted to know about the lifestyle—and I need to know where you're coming from."

Cliff cleared his throat. "Nothing formal—if there is such a thing. A few swats here and there. Uh...holding someone down, restraints. I've watched some, been to a couple of clubs, and here, of course. I've done my homework—a shitload of research. Now

I want more... I want to try the cross and a sling. I couldn't give a shit about the cages or public display. I'm not into degradation or humiliation. Pain only if that's what my sub wants."

"Oh...you already have a sub?"

"No...I'm speaking in general terms."

"Come here. I want to show you something," Draco said. He stood and walked across the thick carpet toward the hidden alcove. Cliff followed, genuinely curious how this former Navy SEAL had come to own a BDSM club.

Draco opened an armoire then stepped back to give Cliff a good look. Many of the items he'd seen in porn, some here at the club and at the two gay clubs he'd visited. "Take a quick look."

Cliff scanned the shelves, before Draco closed the cabinet and turned to face him. "Tell me what you saw."

"Handcuffs—steel, leather, scarves, ropes. Blindfolds, cock rings, dildos, a spreader." Picture-perfect recall was something he'd trained for, but with only a few distracting seconds to look, his memory wasn't perfect. He closed his eyes to visualize the interior of the cabinet. "A feather, a skin mitt, nip rings, cock rings."

"And I assume you're aware there were other items, but those were the ones you easily identified in the limited amount of time I gave you." Draco opened the cabinet again and removed the cuffs and a blindfold. "I'm going to ask you to trust me as I take you through a small exercise."

"What do you have in mind?"

"I want you to strip, then stretch out on the bed."

"I'm—"

"Not for sex—at least not now," Draco said, his voice low. "Think of it as a training exercise, all right? You've survived plenty of those and there is nothing whatsoever you have to fear here...except perhaps a little self-knowledge."

Fear wasn't an issue for Cliff and neither was getting naked in front of another man. He kicked off his shoes, then unfastened his slacks before pushing them and his briefs to the floor. Without hesitation, he raised his shirt over his head, not bothering to unbutton it all the way. With a half-grin, he looked at Draco. "Like what you see?"

Ignoring the question, Draco gestured to the bed. "Stretch out. Give me your right wrist, but keep your left one free for now."

The man had done nothing overtly sexual, yet Cliff's heart rate elevated and his cock went from mildly interested to oh-fuck-yeah. Following the quiet command, Cliff lay back and extended his right arm, which was efficiently cuffed to the wrought iron headboard.

Rather than join him on the bed, however, Draco pulled a spindle-back chair over and sat. "This is a situation that excites you," he said, with a pointed glance at Cliff's hard-as-nails cock.

"Ya think?"

"I do. Now fair warning, bad pop psychology ahead—but I've had a lot of years to observe people, and I've learned a thing or two. SEALs spend a lot of our training in BUDs learning to fight through situations over which we have no control, which is why the training focuses on learning to control our emotions, control our fear. Everything about our jobs is about that control. Sit on the goddamn powder keg full of adrenaline until the last possible second—take the kill, then bug out. There isn't anything we don't want to control. I'll bet even in bed you usually top, right?"

Cliff nodded, but said nothing. Honestly, he couldn't remember the last time he'd bottomed. He didn't hate it, but with the men he'd bedded it hadn't ever been an issue. Wasn't that why he was here? To learn to be a Dom, find a sub?

"It sounds as if you have some vague notion BDSM is something you'd like to try, but when I show you a variety of toys, the first thing your mind latches on to are those involving restraint...another form of control.

"No matter what anyone says, there's no rule book for BDSM. Hell, practitioners can't even all agree on what the letters stand for. In just a few minutes of talking, knowing your background, plus my little pop quiz—completely unscientific, I admit—I think you may find what you're interested in is Dominance and submission. At least starting out.

"The question will be whether you want to maintain that control all the way into the bedroom. Or maybe what you really want is to give up that control for just a little while. A consensual exchange of power that allows you to let someone you trust completely take control of your pleasure. Give me your other hand."

Draco's voice was hypnotic, his words reaching deep inside. Cliff raised his hand, felt the cold circle of steel as the cuff ratcheted around his wrist.

"A good Dom should try everything he plans to do to a sub at least once...but maybe you'll find the temporary role of some relief from the ever-present need for control." Draco stood. "I'm going to leave you here, in the dark for twenty minutes. No one will disturb you, but neither will you be released until I return. Unless of course you want to ring the bell," Draco said, a reference to those in BUDs training who DOR—dropped on request—prior to completion. This little test of Draco's was nothing— twenty minutes of restraint didn't even scratch the surface of how long a SEAL might stay in position waiting for target acquisition. They both knew using a safe word wasn't going to happen—especially not now that the challenge was issued.

Cliff raised his chin in a quick nod and a cocky grin.

Draco chuckled. "And that my friend is why I personally train all the special warfare personnel."

Before Cliff could ask about other SEALs belonging to the club, there was a distant shout that seemed to carry up the stairs over the steady beat of background music.

"Hey, what are you doing?" Cliff recognized Gentry's voice. The hair raised on the back of his neck.

"Let me up," he hissed urgently to Draco. He jerked at the restraints, his need to move having nothing to do with a scene and everything to do with a sense of danger.

"No time. Closing the partition," Draco spoke over him, already moving, one hand going to his pocket and emerging with the remote, the other reaching for his shoulder holster and coming out with a P226 SIG. The bookshelf slid most of the way closed before whirring to a stop after catching on Draco's heel as he stepped out into the office.

Wood splintered as the door to the office was apparently kicked open, and Cliff caught a glimpse of

Draco diving for cover as two shots from the Sig were fired in quick succession.

"What the fuck are you doing? Draco, wa—" Gentry's words were cut off in a hail of automatic gunfire. The sound of wet meat hitting the floor was audible even through the ringing in his ears from the shots. Or maybe it was just his imagination filling in the blanks.

Then the shouting started—the voices rough, the language Spanish.

"Get back, get back."

"Hands in the air. Open the safe, or we wipe out everyone downstairs."

"All right," Draco agreed. "Tell the two assholes with the AK-47s to back the fuck off. Goddamn gangbangers. What the fuck do you think you're going to find—"

"Shut up. Gato, Raul, move back—now. Open the fucking safe, asshole."

"Okay, okay. Nobody else gets hurt..." Something about his tone told Cliff there was probably a weapon inside the safe that Draco believed he could reach before the gunmen fired. There was a brief moment of silence, presumably while Draco worked the lock, then gunfire erupted. A .45 caliber versus automatic weapons. Never a good match.

Straining to see through the narrow opening, Cliff cursed whatever god deemed it amusing to leave him naked and handcuffed to a goddamn bed while three armed gunman attacked less than twenty feet away. Keeping his arms still so the slide of metal against metal didn't draw their attention, Cliff stretched his shoulders and neck to the breaking point, trying to see what he could.

"Goddamn fucker—Raul's down."

"Leave him. Vasquez was right about the fuckin' weapons. Time's up. Grab the money and the backup disc. Get the other 47 and let's go."

For what seemed like an eternity, the silence built and Cliff spent the time cataloging everything he'd seen and heard in the three minutes it had taken for the world to go to hell. When he was certain the shooters were gone, he jerked his wrists hard, testing the strength of the metal and the sturdiness of the bed frame. "Draco? Draco, can you hear me?" Nothing. Not even the sound of labored breathing. Nothing but the ringing in his ears until he finally caught the sound of sirens warbling in the distance, drawing ever closer. Help would come far too late for the men in the other room, but someone with a handcuff key would be here to release him soon. He closed his eyes on a sigh.

Fuck. The only easy day was yesterday. The SEAL motto bounced around in his head before going up in smoke—just like his career.

Chapter Two

Rhino remained frozen in place, his nostrils barely clearing the slimy surface of the swamp that marked the northern boundary of the former Vietnamese concentration camp. The fetid water soaked through to his skin, bringing along a few uninvited guests—probably of the leech variety. Every so often one of them would move, like a cold glob of snot crawling on his leg. It didn't matter. Nothing mattered but remaining in position, out of sight until he had a clear shot.

A shadow passed by the glassless window of the decrepit cinder block building. This might have been a state of the art prisoner holding area in the sixties, but the place had been long abandoned by any official branch of the government. Vines had overgrown most of the structures, reducing them to rubble or shrouding them in a creepy living cloak. A few fence posts had survived the decades, but not with the barbwire attached. The single remaining building was fifteen by eight, with plywood serving as doors, windows, and most of the roof. The three "patriots" who were his targets were holding former Army Ranger Wilton Rufus for the crime of crossing into Viet Nam illegally—which was true—and accusing him of spying for America—which was not true. According to the official government spokesman located in Ho Chi Minh, neither the local police nor the Peoples Army had any knowledge of the American's whereabouts, but if he was discovered, he would be prosecuted for spying.

A second shadow joined the first, and angry voices hung heavy in the air. *Come on, you bastards...step outside. All fucking three of you...step outside...step outside...*

Ordering his mind to go still, Rhino checked his angle once more. Given the layout of the building, the four-by-four-foot bamboo cage housing Sergeant Rufus, and the encroaching jungle, it was the best he could get. His fire team partner Marco Adams—aka Mad Max—was twenty feet to his right, up to his balls in the same swampy shit, but with a less clear shot. He would take anyone Rhino missed. *As if.*

After three days of recon, they'd selected their approach and moved in. Now it was only a matter of minutes...or maybe hours...but either way, the sergeant was going to be heading for home today. All Rhino needed was for the three guards to step through the door—to come clear, so no one took a death shot at Rufus.

As if summoned, guard number three came into view, an automatic rifle slung over one shoulder. He was carrying a metal pie tin of whatever slop they were passing off as food to their prisoner. As he approached the cage, he shouted to the others inside. Rhino didn't have a lot of the language, but enough to catch that the man was calling the others to join him. Something about Rufus's condition made him unhappy, and he wanted an explanation.

Looking straight through the scope at the man he now thought of as target one, Rhino, tightened his grip on his weapon, his finger just a whisper away from taking his shot. From the periphery of his vision, he watched and waited for the others.

Step outside…step outside…

Then the man next to the cage raised his weapon, turning it to point at Rufus, and they were out of time.

Target acquired, Rhino thought as he pressed his finger to the trigger.

Target down.

Panning left, Rhino caught the second man in the throat as he raised his weapon. Number three was a fast little fucker. The man spun at the sound of gunfire, diving for the relative safety of the cinder block as he fired his gun in the direction of the swamp. Rhino caught him in the back of the shoulder and he went down hard, but still moving—for about twenty more seconds. To his right, Mad Max emerged from the swamp like some special effects movie monster. Rhino covered him all the way in, until he received the hand signal that said he was needed to help with Rufus.

It took them less than three minutes to get the skeletal foul-smelling man from the cage, and into the water, heading for home.

Eight hours later, Ryan leaned his head against the vibrating tin can of a transport plane, and closed his eyes. The doc would call him over soon enough, but he'd catch some shut-eye while they worked to stabilize Rufus. He and Marco had done what they could while running through the jungle, taking turns with the man draped over their shoulders. Had they known before the mission how bad his condition was, they might have tried to do things differently...but different took longer, and in this case...longer would have meant dead.

Now, the only thing Ryan wanted was to survive the debrief and the ten days of decompression R and R with the team in Honolulu before they headed back to the unit. Something about this last mission had felt...sour. The trouble wasn't with his team. They were the fucking best...like family. Maybe not quite as much like family as they used to be, but—maybe that was his problem. It just wasn't as much fucking fun with Cliff on shore duty. He gave a little snort. Or maybe he was just pissy after finding a leech on his balls.

"Goddamn bugs," Marco said, digging at his calf. "I want a shower, a twenty-ounce medium rare T-bone from Chow House, and a tight ass riding my cock."

"All at the same time?" Ryan teased.

"Nope. But in that fucking order. How about you?"

"Sorry to break your heart again, Marco, but I keep telling you—I just don't swing that way."

Marco snorted. "As good as. You and Snides are like an old married couple—no wait. I take that back. My parents have been married for thirty years and you two are nothing like them—you guys actually like each other." Marco shifted on the bench, stretching his long legs and crossing them at the ankles.

It wasn't the first time someone commented on his friendship with Cliff Snyder, wondering—or assuming—they were a couple. Their friendship went back twenty years, to BUDs training. The class started with one hundred twenty-four candidates and finished with nineteen. Without a doubt the two of them had spurred each other to success, often side-by-side in the sub-sixty degree water off the coast of San Diego, reminding each other that failure to reach or maintain standards in training meant getting wet—failure on a mission meant death.

For the first few years after qualifying as SEALs, the two of them served on different SEAL teams out of Coronado, but eventually they'd been assigned to the same team and landed on the same platoon many times since.

God…BUDs was forever ago. I'm getting to be an old man in this business.

They'd formed a competitive bond that extended far beyond the already tight connections that SEAL teams develop. The only area their lives didn't intersect was in the bedroom. They each had their own interests there.

"Heard from Snides lately? Man, I thought they'd never get him out of the field. How's he doing at the schoolhouse?" Marco asked, pulling Ryan from his memories.

Ryan laughed and shook his head. "Haven't talked him for a couple weeks, but he wasn't looking forward to this tour of duty. He says it's where old SEALs go to retire."

"He ain't wrong about that," Marco agreed. His mouth quirked up on one side. "So…they cutting you orders there next, old man?"

"Fuck you," Ryan said, laughing. He paused to unwrap a piece of Big Red and folded it into thirds before popping it in his mouth. "All respect to those who teach at BUDs, but, man...I don't think I'm cut out for that training shit. Besides, I don't think they could handle both me and Snides."

Marco punched him on the shoulder before standing as his name was called for his turn with the medical crew. His smile faded. "I hear what you're saying—but don't sell yourself short, Rhino. Despite all the drills, and that invincible feeling you get when you're finished with the training pipeline, you and Cliff got me through the probation period and made sure I stayed alive."

Marco disappeared behind the blue curtain where the medics would conduct their preliminary assessment, and Ryan resumed his head-back-eyes-closed position. Goddamn Marco had called him an old man—and he had the right of it. At least to the kids going through BUDs right now. Only thirty-seven, but twenty years seemed to have passed in the blink of an eye. Now he was in the enviable position of having his reenlistment coincide with negotiating for his next set of orders. Not that there was a lot of wiggle room among their ranks. With less than twenty-five hundred SEALs, the billets were manned with intricate precision. Pay grade, skills, and experience all had to align to meet the mission of the special warfare community. Twenty years also meant he could go home...but other than his Coronado condo, what exactly was home?

Maybe he could skip the mandatory R and R and head straight back to base to talk to the captain and the detailer about his reenlistment options. The powers that be would probably still insist he take some downtime after the mission, but that wouldn't be a problem. He and Snides had the final season of *Sons of Anarchy* on the DVR. The sonofabitch better not have cheated and watched it without him.

*

Ryan eyed the bowl of matchsticks Captain Ross kept on his desk and wondered what the old man would think if he took two to prop up his eyelids. Sure he could function on no sleep for days on end when he was in the field, but for the last—he glanced at the loudly-ticking government-issued Skilcraft clock on the wall—fifty-seven hours, he'd been deloused, debriefed, and determined fit to travel. Returning to San Diego via Yokota, Japan, and Pearl Harbor could take a lot out of a man. He popped in another piece of gum, then leaned back in the chair and concentrated on remaining conscious.

The door clicked open. "Senior Chief Matthews, welcome back," the commanding officer said, stepping through the doorway. Ryan immediately popped to attention and remained in that position. "Carry on, carry on," Captain Ross said absently as he closed the door behind himself and crossed the room to his desk.

Ryan stood until the old man was seated, then resumed his position in the visitor chair situated in front of the flight-deck-sized desk.

"Tell me about the mission, Rhino. Any surprises? Anything we should have done differently?"

Ryan went through the mission, avoiding doing a runaround on his LT by outlining the same key points he'd made during the debrief. The captain listened carefully and made a few notes. Finally, Ross leaned back in his chair and studied Ryan under brows that nearly met over the bridge of his nose.

"Now, what aren't you telling me?"

"Everything worked like clockwork, sir."

"Senior Chief Matthews, I'm not asking you to blow smoke up my skirt—"

"You wear it well, Skipper."

"Smartass. I want to hear the opinion of the senior enlisted man on the mission. How did the platoon respond to Lieutenant Pendergast?"

"You've got a good man—a good leader. I'd go into another mission with him at the helm."

"Good to know. Now what about you? You're here to talk with Petty Officer Harris about orders?"

Ryan weighed his words. "I'm interested in seeing what's available."

The captain nodded. "You're eligible for retirement. You and me have something in common. We've both only got one tour left…"

Deciding to be brutally honest with the man, Ryan shook his head. "I'm not so sure, Skipper. I'm eligible to retire now. I know I stand a good shot at making master chief in the next year or two, but that would mean another three-year enlistment from the date of the promotion—in other words, four or five more years before I could retire. I came to see what kind of orders are available, but it'd have to be something pretty special."

"How about SEAL Team Six?" The captain held out the premier Navy SEAL assignment like some sort of prime bait.

"Is that a genuine offer or are we speculating over what it would take?"

Kincaid smiled. "I think I can manage to drag along one of my best—"

"Hey, congrats, Skipper! You're going to Six—that's a serious honor."

"Yes, it is. It's not my first tour with them, but this one means something special. Senior Chief—if you want those orders, the clock is ticking. All I can do is get you in front of the vetting board—you still have to pass all the interviews and training—and all that takes time. Now, I understand you turned down the decompression R and R at Pearl, which means you have two weeks of mandatory leave starting"—he checked his clock—"in fifteen minutes."

"If you're going to tell me I have fifteen minutes to decide—" His temper rose.

"Hold that thought. What I was going to say is you have until next Friday to decide, and given how short your string is right now, I'd say you need it. If you don't want this DEVGRU special assignment, then I hope you'll consider orders to the Training Command here in Coronado. We need you for one more tour, Senior Chief."

Recognizing dismissal in the captain's tone, Ryan stood. "Sir," he said with a nod.

"Carry on."

Ryan made it to the door, before turning to ask, "Are you taking any others with you, Skipper?"

"I might be considering one or two others. It generally has to be someone within the transfer window. You have me curious, Senior Chief. Is there someone in particular you have in mind?"

"Master Chief Snyder. I know he hasn't been at BUDs that long, but I can give you my unqualified recommendation. He's someone you want on your team."

Captain Ross looked at him for such a long time Ryan began to feel uncomfortable. Did the old man know Snides was gay? Would it really make a difference? Because if so, that was complete bullshit.

Gay or straight didn't matter anymore than black or white when it came to someone having your back on an op. The time came in every career when you needed to consider whether you were willing to do what it took to move up or if you needed to move on...and if the skipper felt that way about a man like Cliff, he could kiss Ryan's ass. He was just about to tell the captain exactly that when the old man heaved a sigh.

"I take it you haven't talk to Snyder since you've been back?"

"No, sir," Ryan answered as the meatball sub he'd had for lunch threatened to make an appearance. He'd been trying to reach Cliff for over forty-eight hours, ever since he'd reach civilization and had his phone back. The asshole wasn't answering his cell or his callback code—which never happened unless he was dark. "Is everything okay?"

"I'm not at liberty to discuss the situation, Senior Chief. Leave it to say the master chief used poor judgment. As much as SEALs look after each other, this isn't something any of us can fix. I suggest you step back and let things run their course. Your leave has officially started. I'll expect to hear from you next Friday. Dismissed."

Chapter Three

Cliff dragged a hand over his hair, not sure he cared for the way it lay smooth across his head instead of brushing flat across the top. Thanks to missions and deployment, he didn't always get to wear his favorite high and tight, but for the better part of twenty-two years—two in the Marines, twenty in the Navy—his cut of choice was shorter than this. With a shrug, he jammed on an old straw hat he'd found last week hanging in the back of the barn and headed out into the pre-dawn morning.

Even at this early hour of the day, his boot heels kicked up dust with every stride. Men spilled from the bunkhouse, making him feel vaguely guilty about taking one of the nicer casitas, but Ty had insisted—and god knew—he was in no position to piss Ty off. The man had provided shelter from the storm, no questions asked.

Despite the circumstances of his being here, there was a bounce in his step as he headed to the barn. As soon as he opened the big door and flipped on the overhead lights, the six or so horses in the barn nickered a greeting from their stalls. "Morning, boys and girls, and uh…" Well, fuck. How exactly did you greet a neutered animal? "Eunuchs…" he finished lamely, then laughed at himself.

First things first. He strolled past each of the horses and scratched a head, rubbed a nose, or tickled an ear, and received several soft horsey snorts of thanks in return. Then for the next little while he busied himself with the routine of the morning. He grabbed the thick hose from the hook on the wall and a feed bucket. Dragging the hose to the first stall, he dropped the pail, opened the latch, and stepped inside. The roan gelding with a white blaze on his nose took a step backward, shaking his head with a snort.

"Morning, Killian." Cliff spent a minute rubbing the horse between his ears then shoved the hose nozzle into the water bucket and turned it on. When it was filled, he turned off the water, stepped out, and latched the stall. "I'll be back with your breakfast in just a minute." The horse nickered as if he understood and Cliff chuckled.

After he repeated the process for all seven stalls on the starboard side of the barn, Cliff went to the feed locker and filled up the bucket. He'd done this job all week. This was a life so different than anything he'd ever known before, and it gave him a small thrill of accomplishment spending an hour with the horses each morning before the other men came in. He'd spent the last two decades either training to kill someone, planning to kill someone, or…well, killing someone. As corny as it sounded…horses didn't judge.

Once Cliff finished doling out all the feed and supplements, he went to the hayloft and threw down a couple bales. Scrambling down the ladder, he cut the twine then stopped to scratch a scruffy black barn cat that head-bumped against his leg. The cat licked his hand then flopped onto the ground and rolled on his back, purring loudly as Cliff scratched his belly.

Straightening, Cliff grabbed up several flakes of hay, the rich alfalfa filling his nostrils and tickling his nose. He looked back through the double-wide door, almost feeling as if someone was watching him— probably because most days the ranch hands would have started to wander in by now, fresh from breakfast and the morning-assignment meeting with Ty's partner, Cass. Apparently, today they were going to be running a little later—probably some new project to plan.

The last time Cliff had visited the Willow Springs Ranch, they'd been in the middle of throwing one heck of a party for some kids with serious illnesses. The way the ranch rallied to give these teens a day to remember had been inspiring. Even a famous country music star, Brody Kent, had shown up. In a roundabout way, it was thanks to Brody that Cliff was out here right now. If Whit had still been working at the WSR instead of building his own place with Brody, Cliff couldn't have taken over some of the other man's duties. Not that he was anywhere close to qualified to be a ranch hand, but dammit, look how far he'd come in just a week.

Making another round through the stalls to give each horse a share of the alfalfa, he also checked out the floor conditions and decided they could wait to be cleaned until after the horses and their late-for-work riders headed out for the morning. Time enough for him to go for a ride. He led Killian to the crosstie area and fastened his harness before going to the tack room. Grabbing the bridle and hefting the saddle onto his shoulder, he returned to Killian and balanced the saddle on the sawhorse. The big gelding stood patiently, and hopefully not remembering how slow and awkward Cliff had been the first few times he'd saddled him up. Walking to the horse's head, he murmured a few words as he got the bridle situated in his hand. He pinched Killian's upper lip to slide the bit gently between his teeth. After it was positioned, he pulled the straps up over the horse's cheeks and ears, then patted the side of his face.

"Hey, we're getting better at this every day, huh?"

"It sure looked to me like you knew what you were doing."

Ryan.

Cliff closed his eyes and rested his forehead against Killian's neck. He'd known this day was inevitable...but dayum. Did it have to come so soon? He turned and looked up to where the voice had come from.

Grabbing the edge of the platform with both hands, Ryan swung over and dropped in one easy motion, landing on the dirt with a thud. The horses in the stalls on either side of him shuffled back, and one huffed a snort in his direction.

"Ty?" Cliff finally forced himself to ask. He reached for the saddle blanket and spread it across the horse's back, smoothing and adjusting each wrinkle away.

"Yeah...took me a while though. Don't ever go dark on me again—"

Cliff turned away and Ryan broke off. He didn't have to look to know that his friend's lips would be pressed together in a tight line. It was the look he always got when people pissed him off.

Well, that was too bad. Cliff wasn't exactly a happy camper either. He'd probably have to kick Ty's ass over this. Goddamn. What really pissed him off was how easy it had been for Ry to get a drop on him. He'd known that platform was there, had even looked on top of it on his first trip to the WSR—but this morning? He'd been up and down the ladder to the hayloft more than a dozen times this past week, and had only looked at the platform on the first trip. After that? It had become invisible—nothing to worry about. Apparently not even when his subconscious tried to warn him he was being watched. That was the kind of lazy shit that could get you killed when you were a SEAL. Except he *wasn't* anymore, was he?

Ryan stayed behind him without speaking, so Cliff continued saddling Killian. He folded the leather stirrups over the top of the saddle and lifted the whole thing onto the horse's back, raising and lowering it, then twisting and sliding until the saddle and blanket aligned smoothly, exactly where he wanted it. He gave it a few hard thunks with his fists, then reached under the horse's belly, his fingers moving confidently over the buckles and cinches.

"You look like you're going somewhere," Ryan finally said. "How come I didn't know you could ride a horse? You look like a goddamn cowboy."

"Killian is expecting a ride, and I plan to give him one." Cliff finally straightened, then turned and looked directly at Ryan. A couple of inches shorter and twenty-five pounds lighter, people seeing them together might think that Cliff was the more dangerous of the two—but looks could be deceiving. Ryan's hazel eyes were muddy today, underscored with dark smudges, deep as bruises. His face was thin, his dark blond hair shaggy, his muscles tense, hard—

all familiar post-mission—but usually shit that eased itself off during the ten-day decompression duty. "You look like shit, Rhino. Everything okay? When did you get back?"

Ryan frowned. "What day is this?"

"Sunday."

Ryan nodded. "Okay…that makes sense, I think. I got CONUS on Thursday, saw the old man Friday. Called Ty yesterday. Here I am."

Cliff narrowed his eyes. "Where's the rest of your team, Rhino?"

He shrugged. "Pearl. I'm bored with Hawaii—had some shit to do. No worries, I'm on leave for the next two weeks. Same as…"

Cliff knew Ryan meant taking leave was the same as the decompression with his team, but it wasn't. Not really. Sometimes though, you just needed some downtime away from those who thought they knew you best.

"I don't suppose if I told you I was okay, you'd go away and leave me the fuck alone?"

Ryan stared for half a second, then turned on his heel. For a fleeting instant, Cliff thought he might have dodged the bullet that was his best friend's wrath. Then Ryan flipped him the bird as he stalked toward the barn doors. "I'm grabbing some food and then a few hours of shut-eye. You better be fucking prepared to talk when I wake up."

Cliff rolled his eyes at the dramatic exit. He put his foot into the stirrup, stepped up, and swung his leg over the saddle. With a squeeze of his knees, he urged Killian outside and headed east. As he passed the main house, he caught sight of Ty, arms folded across his chest as he leaned in the doorway wearing his favorite uniform: a white apron over a white T-shirt and worn blue jeans. The former Navy SEAL scowled at him. Raising his hand to the brim of his hat, he inclined his head in Ty's direction. Then he followed Rhino's example, lowered his index finger and flipped him off before kicking Killian into a canter. It was going to be a long fucking day.

****

Ryan had watched Cliff from his perch in the top of the barn for as long as he'd dared, but once it looked as if Cliff planned to go for a ride, he'd made himself known and dropped to the floor for a rather anticlimactic reunion. He'd arrived an hour earlier and, just as Ty suggested, he'd used the ladder to the loft, then swung from the beams like a kid on the monkey bars until reaching the center of the barn. Some time in the distant past, a kind soul had layered plywood over a twenty-foot section of crossbeams to create a sturdy platform, probably for storage. Whatever the original intention, the dust-covered surface had been ideal for remaining out of sight while watching Cliff do what Ty had referred to as his morning chores.

Cliff had looked tired, but the tightness around his eyes and the creases etched around his mouth told him this was more than a physical exhaustion. Something big was eating at his friend. Well— welcome to the club, Ryan thought, watching as Cliff saluted Ty, then kicked the horse into a run. Damn...he does look like a cowboy—from the tight Wranglers to the dusty boots and a beat up straw hat on his head. *What the fuck?*

"You going to stand there watching all day or come in and get something to eat?" Ty asked. The man had moved closer than he should have been able to without Ryan noticing. Damn, he *was* tired.

"Gotta place for me to crash?"

"Yep...soon as you eat. Follow me, and let's get these ranch hands outta here, Cass has held 'em up long enough."

"You're a goddamn mother hen," Ryan groused, but the smell of coffee and bacon could overcome any reluctance.

"Cluck, cluck," Ty said. "You get a free pass on the boots-off-at-the-door policy on your first visit. Now sit." He pointed to a stool pulled up to a stainless steel workstation in the large kitchen. Ty poured a mug of coffee and put it in Ryan's hand, then piled bacon, eggs, and hash browns on a plate. He set the food and some toast in front of Ryan, but for the next several minutes, conversation was impossible. A stream of men wandered through the kitchen, rinsing their plates and loading them directly into the dishwasher. They alternately gave Ty shit or praised the last meal...or the next. Finally, a long, tall drink of cowboy sauntered through the arched doorway that opened into the dining room. He carried a serving platter that was empty, save the tongs.

"Sorry, honey. I tried to save you a sausage," the man said, his brows raised high, giving him a picture of innocence that Ryan didn't buy.

Ty frowned and studied the other man for a long moment. "Huh. Guess I'll top tonight then."

Laughing, the man, who must be Ty's partner, Cass, placed the platter in the sink, then stepped close to cup Ty's face in his hands. "Gotta run. I'll see you in a couple of hours." He lowered his mouth and took a long kiss.

Ryan wasn't a complete stranger to guy-on-guy PDA, but it wasn't something he was used to seeing so up close and personal. He looked down at his empty plate, telling himself it was to cede them some privacy. After a moment though, his gaze was drawn upward. There was something comfortable about the way they fit together. Both men were big. Ty was broad, his shoulders and arms bulky in the tight T-shirt. Cass was taller, lean and lanky, but his forearms were heavily corded, no doubt from years of ranch work. The two men pressed close, hips aligned, chest-to-chest, tongues clearly engaged as the kiss spun out…and damn if Ryan's dick didn't twitch. Amazing what six months of abstinence could do for you…just about anything looked good.

Cass stepped back, and they smiled at each other before he turned toward the back door. Two steps later, he spun around.

"Shit, where're my manners?" He strode toward Ryan, his hand extended. "I'm Cass Cartwright. Welcome to the Willow Springs Ranch."

"Thanks, appreciate it. I'm Ryan Matthews. Nice to meet you."

They shook hands, then Cass stepped toward the door once more.

"Sorry, I really do need to get out there, but I'm sure we'll have plenty of time to talk later." He stuck a tan felt cowboy hat on his head and shot a grin at Ty. "Be good." He turned his smile on Ryan, who found himself grinning back.

"You might as well go ahead and do whatever it is Ty has in mind. He won't give up until you do." Cass's laughter followed him out the door.

"Huh. You have plans for me?"

"No doubt. But first, how the hell are you? You just came off mission but no R and R with your platoon?"

Ryan shrugged. "I'm rotating off the team. Wanted to come back to talk about orders, maybe look at a few options."

"You here to give Cliff shit about what happened?"

Ryan did a slow blink, wishing he had a least one fucking piece of the puzzle. "Probably—only I don't *know* what happened."

It was Ty's turn to blink. "Then why were you looking for him?"

"Uh…hello? Cliff's been my best friend for twenty years," Ryan said. Frustration welled up and threatened to spill over. He gestured at Ty. "We might not know each other well, but don't make the mistake of thinking you're the only friend Cliff has. Now I've been in CONUS less than a hundred hours, and I'm trying to find out what the fuck is going on."

Ty looked at him a long time, and Ryan hid a sigh. The man across the counter from him was a certified hero, and even if they never served on the same SEAL team together, he was a former teammate of Cliff's—someone he'd trusted enough to help him go dark. And someone who knew enough about their friendship that when Ryan had called—Ty'd told him how to find Cliff. He took a deep breath and let it out slowly.

"I've been in Afghanistan for the last six months. We got add-on orders on our way home. The mission took a platoon of us to Southeast Asia. We had a debrief"—he tried to count back the days but gave up and went for general information—"earlier this week. The rest of the guys remained in Pearl for decompression, but I came home, like I said. I arrived sometime in the middle of the night on…Thursday?" He nodded to himself. "I talked to the CO on Friday about some new orders. When I mentioned something about taking Snides along, he warned me off—said the master chief used poor judgment and to leave it alone.

"Now, by that time, my ass was more than dragging, but I called Cliff's contact phone—and got nothing back. I called a mutual friend at BUDs, and he said Cliff was on emergency leave—he thought his mother was having surgery. It was like playing connect the dots. Of course when I called Steve—Cliff's dad—to ask about Carly, he said she was fine and they hadn't heard from Cliff for a couple of weeks.

"Ty—I am tired, but I'm not stupid. Rather than raising an alarm that Cliff might not appreciate by calling more contacts in the Coronado area, I tried to think who he'd reach out to outside the active duty community."

Ty nodded. "Which led to me—"

"Well, especially since he'd been out here not too long ago."

Standing suddenly, Ty stretched out a hand and pulled Ryan to his feet. "Okay, that works for me. Since I gather from Snide's reaction, he's not overly pleased with either of us at the moment…" His lips twitched as if he was fighting a smile. "Go catch some zees. The casita's unlocked, just pull your Jeep around."

"Wait. What? Which casita? And what the fuck is going on with Cliff?"

The twitch turned into a full-on smile. "And you call yourself special ops? The casita with Cliff's Jeep in front of it…you know, the one that looks a helluva lot like yours? There's a spare bedroom. And as for what's going on? That's not my story to tell."

Chapter Four

Flipping on the lights and banging on the door, Cliff yelled, "Hey, Rhino, wake up, time to go…"

Ryan bolted upright, his hand wrapped around the handle of his throwing knife. His eyes locked on the target Cliff made in the doorway. For half a second, he wasn't sure Ryan would put it together quickly enough—which would leave Cliff with his hands full of an angry Rhino—or a blade in his chest.

"Cliff?" Ryan said, his knuckles white on the balanced steel. "What's…uh…*shit.*"

He rubbed a hand over his face, then cleared his throat. "Jesus, Cliff. You fucking trying to commit suicide?" He dropped the knife onto the bedside table with a thud.

"Come on, sleepyhead, you've slept all day, they're expecting us at the main house for the party."

Without any further explanation, Cliff turned away and was halfway to the kitchen when the faint brush of breeze warned him of the attack half a breath before Ryan slammed into him. He whirled, riding Rhino's momentum, absorbing the blow and driving the smaller man into the wall. In the narrow space, and with his bigger size, Cliff would have the advantage for a few minutes, now that the surprise part of the attack was over. Unless Rhino had a weapon. Since he wasn't already bleeding, chances were better than average he'd left the knife on the table.

"Hey, Ry...man, come on," he said softly, just in case he'd triggered a flashback instead of just pissing the man off. He pressed his forearm against Ryan's chest, Cliff felt like an ass. "Ryan, come on, are you with me? I'm sorry, that was a shitty thing to do to you—*unh*." Cliff grunted as Ryan head-butted him, catching him on his left cheekbone.

"Ow...hey. Stop it."

"Goddamn right it was a shitty thing to do," Ryan spat, shoving away from Cliff and stalking back to his bedroom...naked. Cliff had to close his eyes to keep from staring at those tight, muscled globes bunching and stretching as Ryan retreated. Damn...some things were hard to unsee.

Moving to the kitchen to make a cup of coffee because despite the mid-afternoon time on the clock, Ryan did just wake up, he ground the beans, popped the reusable filter into the Keurig, and set it for strong. By the time Ryan appeared—fully clothed in a faded gray T-shirt and worn button-front jeans, his bare feet sticking out from the frayed hems—two cups of coffee were on the table.

Grabbing a banana from the bowl on the counter, Ryan peeled it open and popped half in his mouth before he pulled out one of the heavy ladder-back chairs and joined him at the table. Watching Cliff the whole while, he swallowed the banana, before taking a sip of coffee. Staring back, Cliff waited him out.

"Asshole."

"Yeah," Cliff agreed. "I had the stupid idea in my head if I could piss you off enough, you might let it go until later. I forgot what a stubborn ass you are."

"What a stubborn ass *I* am? What about the time you—no wait—you are not going to sidetrack this conversation. When I couldn't find you after the skipper's cryptic remarks, I was mildly concerned—but to go fucking dark? Without even leaving me a way to reach you? Now you've got me scared. No bullshit here, Cliff. Will you tell me what in the fuck is going on with you?"

"What did they say at the base?"

"*Say?* They think your mom had surgery. Carly says hello by the way."

"You talked to my *mom?* For fuck's sake—I'm forty years old. Why would you do that?"

"Cliff, listen to me, will you? The only thing I know is the old man said you'd exhibited an unfortunate lack of judgment. That's fucking it.

Charlie over at BUDs said you went on emergency leave. I don't have a fucking clue why you're here, or what you think everyone at the base knows, but man, you better start talking because otherwise I'm going to kick your ass."

"As if. At least not until you finish your first cup of coffee."

Ryan didn't even crack a smile at the long-running joke. They stared at each other for a full sixty clicks of the kitchen wall clock, then with a sigh that seemed to start somewhere in his boots, Cliff gave in. "I royally fucked up, Ry. Bad enough that it's cost me everything."

"What? Tell me what it is you think is so bad? I mean seriously, what's the worst? They cut you loose from BUDs and you go back to a team?"

"Not even close. My retirement papers are already processing. And I'm probably fucking lucky I get to keep that."

"Bullshit—Cliff, you're killing me. I can't even in my wildest imagination come up with anything you'd do that would merit forcing you to retire...you're just not that guy."

Raising his mug, Cliff bought a final few seconds. He'd rather lie down in a bed of fire ants than admit what he'd done, but to hell with it. He'd lain in a lot a shit over the years—Ryan would probably laugh his fucking ass off, then go back to the Navy, and Cliff could stop worrying about it. Mostly.

"You know your friend Draco?"

"At Hard Labour?" Ryan blinked.

Cliff snorted. "How many Draco's do you know? And fictional characters don't count."

Leaning back in his chair, Ryan crossed his ankle over one knee and draped an arm over the back of the chair. Cliff recognized the open and relaxed pose for what it was. His friend was telegraphing his willingness to listen.

"Okay, so you know I've been hanging around you too long, because your, uh…interest in domination is, uh…mildly interesting. Except in a way that doesn't involve tits and shit."

At that, Ryan laughed. "Tits? Come on, I bet they're as many gay men sporting tit rings as there are straight women."

"Holy shit, I hope I find them soon, 'cause that's fuckin' hot." They shared a smile, and just for a moment, Cliff wondered if just maybe everything could work out. Not the Navy—done was done—but maybe he and Ryan could still hang out when he wasn't out of CONUS.

"I asked Draco to talk with me a little about getting more involved, on what he would recommend. Beyond just coming to the club regularly, I mean."

"You could have asked me, you know," Ryan said quietly.

"Uh...hello? You've been gone for six months. I don't know what's wrong, Ry. I'd have talked to you when you got here, but I've been so fucking restless, you know?"

"The assignment to BUDs school?"

"Yeah, I think so. The guys are great—hell, I think we both know almost all of them—but I just wasn't getting the same satisfaction from having a daily routine. I know that doesn't make much sense, because on team we train every day when we aren't deployed—but there was always that sense of building something that I'm just not getting.

"Hell, maybe it's just too much time on my hands. Anyway...this idea has been growing for a while now—that something's...missing." Afraid he might be revealing too much of himself, Cliff looked up and caught nothing but empathy on his friend's face.

"And the idea of finding someone who fits you is appealing—and given the shitload of BDSM buzz in the media and fiction, it always sounds like the Dom finds the perfect sub and they complete each other," Ryan guessed.

"Shit. When you say it like that it sounds stupid, but yeah, something like that. Maybe when you're hanging around I don't notice it so much, because there's always someone to work out with or catch a movie or whatever—but, man, when you were deployed this last time and I was stuck on shore duty, I just couldn't shake the boredom."

Ryan finished off his coffee. "Okay, you went to see Draco. Nothing to get the Navy too bent. What happened?"

"I went to the club…flirted with the new bartender—a dude named Gentry—then went to Draco's office. We talked for a bit, what he said…I don't know how much I bought into it for a long-term thing for me, but I won't deny it was hot. He's got a bed in his office, so one thing led to another—"

"Whoa—steer left of the TMI if you're getting ready to tell me who topped and bottomed," Ryan laughed.

Cliff's cheeks heated. He stood, pushing his chair back hard enough it almost clattered over. "Hey, shit—I forgot. Ty's waiting for us. We gotta—"

Ryan was in his face in a nanosecond, backing him up against the counter. A part of Cliff welcomed the aggressive contact, was tempted to pick Ryan up and carry his pit bull ass outside so they could spend an hour beating the shit out of each other. Maybe then his brain would stop itching with all the thoughts that had been keeping him awake. Before he could act on the thought, Ryan tugged on his arm, dragging him toward the couch.

"No—shit—you're not going anywhere, Cliff. Goddammit, I shouldn't have said that. I was being a smartass… Okay, so you let him fuck you. Seriously, no big deal."

"No, actually we didn't fuck." Cliff shrugged, then turned to face the darkened television. "I can't say we wouldn't have—things never got that far." He gave the information like it was a briefing. The handcuffs, the three gangbangers, Gentry and Draco—and his total failure to do anything except lay there like a fucking victim while the bad guys took out innocents.

"Aww…shit," Ryan said when he finally stopped speaking.

"Yeah." Cliff snorted. "That about sums it up. Of course the fun was only just starting," he said, bitterness lacing every word. "Fucking first cops on the scene thought it was a riot to catch a gay Navy boy all trussed up. It would have been worse if they'd known I was special ops, but the gray hair threw them off that scent. Of course once the detectives arrived and the serious questioning started, they got my command—so it's not like I could have avoided it forever. Once I made it out of the PD, I went straight to the commanding officer and told him everything."

"You fucking noble—"

"Ryan, I had to tell him. I'm a witness, I saw these guys—the two that got away. I've spent hours poring over mug shots, making statements, all kinds of shit.

Supposedly, the real target was the club records, and these guys got away with the backup files. I have no idea how current anything is they took, but that's why the DA is all over me—to keep me isolated from the rest of the investigation so there's no chance of contamination—her words, not mine. She wants me in some local's version of witness protection until the killers are ID'd. Trust me when I tell you there wasn't a chance in hell of keeping this from the Navy—and goddammit—the skipper deserved to hear it from me first."

Nodding, Ryan reached into his pocket and pulled out a crumpled foil-wrapped stick of Big Red. After removing the wrapper, he popped it in his mouth, the scent of cinnamon filling the air as he started to chew. Still saying nothing, he leaned forward, elbows on his knees, hands clasped. Classic *'Rhino thinking'* posture.

Taking advantage of the moment, Cliff stood and went to the kitchen, returning a few minutes later with four opened bottles of Corona. He set three bottles on the table, then drank deeply of the fourth.

Ryan raised a brow. "Are we getting drunk?"

"Maybe. Told you we were late for the party. I figured we could start here and take the other two to-go."

"What party? Is somebody celebrating?"

"No doubt someone is, but not the Chargers fans. The Pats and the Seahawks are in—the damn commercials better be good." Cliff tilted his head back to drain the bottle.

"The commercials—oh shit. It's Super Bowl Sunday? Well tie me up and call me bad," Ryan said, his face perfectly composed as he stared at the bottles. "Oh wait—that's your role." He looked up, his mouth twitching at the corner as he fought the laugh.

Cliff lowered his bottle and blinked. He couldn't believe his best friend had the balls to say something like that. His lip started to curl as a spasm rippled across his stomach muscles. Without further warning, beer spewed as the laugh he'd momentarily fought won out over swallowing.

Ryan's eyes went wide as the spray of Corona went everywhere, including over his shirt. Then the two of them lost it, laughing until they were both gasping for air.

"I can't believe—" Cliff started, but broke off as another fit of laughter nearly doubled him over.

"Oh my god…" Ryan looked down at his splattered shirt. "You are such a pig." The effect was ruined when he snorted at his own joke.

The knock at the door didn't even slow them down as Ty stepped inside. "I thought the party was at my place— Oh, are we having a wet T-shirt contest?"

Laughing even harder, Ryan slid off the couch, knocking his elbow into a bottle of beer, and then catching it before it could tumble over. Cliff sucked in a huge breath, forcing a fragile calm he wasn't sure he could maintain.

"Sorry, Ty—we'll clean up and be right there," Cliff offered, his voice wavering with more suppressed laughter.

Still chuckling and wiping the tears from his eyes, Ryan nodded. "Yeah…right there. Sorry, man…Cliff got tied up." The bottle landed on the table with a thunk, barely remaining upright, as Ryan fell over sideways onto the floor, clutching his stomach as a fresh bout of laughter seized him.

Ty's gaze flickered to Cliff, who was barely holding it together. "Glad to see you have this all straightened out, see you soon." Ty backed out of the door, smiling and looking as if he was fighting his own laughter.

Feeling lighter than he had in days, Cliff reached out his hand, and Ryan accepted the help up. "Come on, Rhino, before Cookie gets pissed and we don't get any of the ribs he's grilling."

"Yeah…no sense in letting a little thing like this Dominate our evening…"

Cliff rolled his eyes, before giving in and joining the laughter once again.

****

Ryan munched on a rib and watched the other men as they moved comfortably around the living room of the main ranch house. Ty and Cass were relaxed hosts, expecting everyone to help themselves. The dining room table and sideboard were practically groaning with platters of ribs and wings, and a build-your-own-taco bar. Periodically, Ty would disappear for a few minutes, then return with some new goodie...like the layered chili and beef nachos that appeared at the beginning of the second quarter or the delicious potato skins that showed up between the halftime show and the talking heads over-analyzing every detail of the game as if world domination were at stake.

Beyond the hot food there were veggie trays, chips, salsa...even a frijole clam dip that Cliff swore was to die for. Ryan would take his word on it. There were too many other goodies to take a chance on fishy beans...but no matter what Ty brought out, the men just kept eating. Twenty-one of them, in fact. He knew...he'd counted.

Black, white, Hispanic, tall, short, slender, husky, bald, long-haired, blonds, brunettes, even a redhead. What there *wasn't* was a woman. Not one.

Men held hands, or sat next to each other on the sofas or floor pillows. No one thought anything about a kiss or a pat. Or a nothing. He and Cliff weren't the only men in the group not touching each other romantically. Even as the evening wore on and the drinking and trash talk escalated, it was clear that not everyone was paired up and no one gave a good goddamn one way or the other.

"Oh, no!" Cliff groaned along with half the men there as the Seahawks' receiver let a ball slip through his hands. "This is going to require copious amounts of booze to get through."

Cliff patted Ryan's thigh, pushed himself from the couch, and stalked into the kitchen. Ryan's gaze followed him out the door, then he caught a movement from the corner of his eye and he discovered Ty watching him watch Cliff. Ty raised his bottle in a silent toast, before turning back to his lover, and whispering something that made the other man smile. Ryan wished he knew what the toast was for.

Replaying the scene through someone else's eyes, he realized he and Cliff looked as much like a couple as many of the pairs here. They sat jammed hip-to-hip on the crowded sofa, smacking each other on the shoulder or leg, bringing each other drinks, making small inside jokes, their laughter private.

Just like they'd done at dozens of football parties over the years. Or beach parties. BUDs graduation parties. End of mission parties. Hell…he couldn't remember the last party he'd been to without Cliff. Cliff rented an apartment in the same complex as

Ryan's condo. They even DVR'd their favorite shows to watch together. They knew each other's secrets.

No wonder Marco said they acted like an old married couple—they practically were.

Cliff returned, carrying a dark bottle of beer in one hand and a fishbowl masquerading as a margarita in the other. He handed the icy concoction to Ryan before he squeezed into the spot on the couch between Ryan and an old rodeo cowboy named Jesse.

"Holy shit, if I drink another one of these, you might as well pour me into a tub and cart me home."

"Hah. You must be getting old, then. I've never seen a couple of margaritas put you under any table." Cliff bumped his shoulder. "Seriously, you okay?" he asked quietly. "We can go if you want. I know your ass must be dragging."

"Nah...I'm good. At least until I finish this." He raised the glass, took a swallow, then squinted at the television. "Jesus, please tell me the game clock is blurry? Is that a six or an eight?"

Cliff laughed. They'd been doing a lot of laughing over the last few hours...it felt good. "It's three minutes, forty seconds."

Ryan did a triple take, before his eyes convinced his brain that Cliff was jerking his chain.

"Shit...you nearly had me. It's eight minutes. God...I thought my eyes really lost it there. Would make the offer from the Skipper pretty easy to turn down if I couldn't pass the physical." As soon as the words left his mouth, Ryan wanted them back. He could only hope Cliff was too involved in the game to pay much attention.

"Yeah? What orders are those?"

"Eh…it's nothing I want to talk about tonight. Let's concentrate on the end of the game—and then tomorrow I plan to sleep for twenty-four straight."

Cliff shook his head. "I heard you straight boys like to sleep. Sad. Really sad. And Rhino…congratulations, man. No one deserves Six more than you."

Ryan swallowed half his drink in his surprise. "How did you—shit, you didn't know. You guessed."

"An educated guess. Not much other reason for you to have a one-on-one with the man just selected to head up DEVGRU—he'd want you for Six. It makes sense. You're the goddamn best," Cliff said, his voice was a quiet growl in its intensity. "The goddamn best."

Chapter Five

Cliff stumbled a little in the dark of his bedroom, reluctant to turn on the lights and ruin his night vision. It had been a long while since he'd had so much to drink—or felt so relaxed. There was definitely something to be said about being on the WSR, away from anyone who might know him or what he did for a living.

In their careers, it was conceivable they could be targeted for one of their field actions or just by virtue of being Navy SEALs. Just like the cops who'd enjoyed harassing him once they'd discovered his profession. Some people needed to try to knock down others to feel good about themselves. But here? He and Ryan were just a couple more guys.

He stripped to his boxers and tossed his jeans onto the chair before pulling back the covers on the king-sized bed. A shudder raced up his spine, and for just a moment, he remembered the frustration and helplessness of the situation when he'd been trapped on the other bed...listening to those fucking punks. His stomach clenched at the thought of Gentry and

Draco. Their bodies had been removed by the time the cops saw fit to release him from the alcove, but he'd never forget listening to their last moments or the blood that soaked the floor when he'd been led through the office to the stairs. Ryan would eventually ask for details about how they died—especially Draco, since they'd been friends—but they'd both learned to compartmentalize death a long time ago.

That didn't mean they weren't affected by loss, but there was a time and a place to mourn, to say good-bye, and it wasn't while the battle raged. Despite several warnings from the DA and lead investigator, Cliff would like nothing more than to hunt down those gangbangers and make them pay...and Ryan would be more than happy to help. He recognized the danger in those thoughts, as well.

Blowing out a breath at the loss of his mellow mood of a few minutes ago, Cliff moved silently on bare feet to open the bedroom door and listened. The quiet murmur of television voices from behind Ryan's door would mask any noise he might make. Hell, Rhino was probably passed out on his bed already.

Cliff padded to the refrigerator, considered then dismissed the idea of another beer. He had a long drive ahead of him in the morning. Grabbing a bottle of water instead, he drank half down in one long pull.

Turning, he found Ryan standing near the counter, watching him. With the moonlight streaming in through the window providing the only illumination, his friend's face was difficult to read, but his naked body was a little hard to miss.

"Want some?" Cliff held the bottle of water in Ryan's direction.

With a nod, Ryan took the bottle and finished it off. With a perfect aim, even in the near total darkness, he tossed the empty into the wastebasket. "And the crowd goes wild."

"Idiot," Cliff said, opening the fridge for two more bottles of water. Once again passing a bottle to Ryan, he started to head back to the bedroom. Ryan's hand on his arm stopped him.

"I...uh...had a good time tonight." Ryan's words weren't slurred, but there was a lazy cadence beneath the stilted delivery that spoke of too much tequila.

"Yeah, me too. Ty and Cass are good folk. They've made this place a good home for a lot of guys who needed a fresh start."

"Is that what you're thinking of doing? A fresh start out here as some kind of cowboy? 'Cause, man...I could see the attraction. You out here surrounded by all those hot guys—I mean obviously not the couples, but there were at least half of them in there single, right?"

Cliff laughed softly at Ryan's concern for his love life. "Yeah...sorry about that. I didn't even think about how you might have felt...surrounded by all those guys." He studied Ryan's face. "You weren't offended, right? I mean you've been to gay clubs with me and it's never bothered you…"

"Offended? Nah…why would I be? You never were offended at the straight clubs, right?" His hand tightened on Cliff's forearm, and he seemed to weave a little on his feet.

"Hey, Rhino, come on. You need to get some sleep—"

"Are we having a bromance?" Ryan blurted.

"A bromance?" Cliff laughed, and Ryan's eyes narrowed. Oh boy, never laugh at a drunk who thinks he's making an important point.

"Yeah, a bromance. Where two guys hang out all the time, like the same shit, would probably fuck each other if they were both gay—or if one of them was female."

Fighting off more laughter, Cliff nodded. "Sure, you can call it that. Come on, princess, let's get you to bed."

Ryan didn't yield when Cliff tried to pull his arm free in order to lead him toward the bedrooms. "What do you think? Should I take the orders?"

"What, are you nuts? You've been waiting for those orders your whole career."

"Yeah, that's the problem…my whole career."

"What the hell does that mean?"

"You're not the only one eligible to retire. Just because you had two years prior service in the Marines before you joined the Navy, you've got more time in service than me, but yeah…it's been twenty years this month. I don't know if I want one more tour. That's another four or five years, in order to retire at the new pay grade I'd no doubt pick up in the next year or two.

"True, but it's also more money when you do retire. And, Rhino…it's *Six*." He referred to the DEVGRU unit by their unofficial name, hoping to jar a little sense into his friend.

Squeezing his arm a little, Ryan leaned in, as if imparting a great secret. "You should be there."

Cliff shook his head. "That's done. We don't even need to think about it. I just gotta figure what I want to do next."

"See, Snides…that's the thing. If I have to wait another four or five years before I retire and you move on, you're going to get too fucking far ahead. I don't like that. 'Sides, that'd mean no more football or watching *NCIS*. You'd get to see all the episodes of *So You Think You Can Dance* without me telling you how gay that is."

"Ha, now I know you're drunk. We only watch that because you like the women's skimpy outfits. You probably need to quit hanging out with me and spend the next six months of your training cycle finding the right little woman and getting laid on a regular basis. Hell, get a wife! Then you'll be all set for retirement when you're done with the next tour. She can cook your sorry ass dinner, wash your clothes… Yep…you need a wife."

"Fuck that shit. I'd sooner fuck you than ever get married again. In fact—"

Time seemed to stop, as if they both needed a moment to absorb the truth of those words.

"Careful what you wish for, Ryan," Cliff said, his voice a ragged whisper. His cock went rock hard, ignoring every warning he could throw out that this wasn't going to happen. Ryan was drunk, and they both were horny, but this was a line neither of them needed to cross. Too much was at stake for a little temporary relief. Guilt and regret could kill a friendship.

Even as all the reasons they needed to walk away raced through his mind, the moment stretched. For once Cliff had no idea what Ryan was thinking. Cliff started to pull his arm away again. Rhino shifted his grip and guided their joined hands to brush over Ryan's hard cock.

"Not going here with you, Ry. Not worth a friendship."

"Won't cost anything. You weren't wrong to try it, you know."

"Try? What are you—"

Ryan's hand closed around Cliff's erection. "To try a little bondage. To let someone else take control."

Cliff jerked his hips to free his cock. "Is that what you think? That I enjoyed lying there while—"

"Don't be stupid, Cliff. Of course not—not that night—not there. But here? Oh yeah…suck my cock, baby. Come on, we both want this tonight."

Ryan didn't know what the fuck he was talking about. Sure Cliff had been at Draco's to find out more about the lifestyle. Ryan above everyone should know that even though they played on different teams, they were both dominant men, both used to being in absolute control. He had to make Ryan shut up, to stop this foolishness before he said things they'd both regret come morning.

Twisting roughly away, he body slammed Ryan against the wall. A small smile lingered over the other man's mouth, and Cliff bent in, not to taste it, and definitely not to feel those familiar lips pressed against his…but to wipe away the knowing, mocking smile.

Their mouths crashed together, a fusion of teeth and tongues, of malty beer and tart tequila, and an underlying touch of cinnamon. With his hands pressed to the wall on either side of Ryan's head, Cliff leaned down, taking advantage of their height difference. Ryan's face tilted up, his hands sliding over Cliff's bare chest to pinch his nipples.

Ahhh...he wanted to shout. Fire raced through his nerves as the little buds burned and the heat streaked straight to his cock and tightened his balls. Ryan took advantage of Cliff's momentary distraction and snaked an arm up, his fingers twisting in Cliff's hair and holding him tight while he plundered Cliff's mouth. With his pulse thundering erratically, he lost himself in Ryan's kiss. Closing his eyes, he leaned into Ryan, their hips brushed together and a hard cock pressed against his. Ryan's tongue slid over Cliff's, teased the roof of his mouth, teeth scraping over lips. Cliff moaned as desire built.

Ryan gave another hard tweak to his nip then scraped his nails through Cliff's chest hair and up to his shoulder to apply a not-so-subtle downward pressure. Using his hair like a handle, he pulled Cliff's head back from the kiss.

"Now, Cliff, baby. I want you on your knees." He released Cliff's hair and started pressing down. "You've always said no one can give a better blow job than another man...show me."

They were almost the same height, just a couple of inches separating them, but right now, the way Rhino looked at him, pushed at him to drop to his knees and bend to his will, was fucking sexy. The two of them had been friends for twenty years, yet this was a road they'd never even remotely discussed traveling together.

A distant part of his mind sensed the danger, worried their friendship wouldn't survive the morning light if he capitulated, but damn... Cliff had never seen Ryan like this. Commanding bordering on arrogant? Sure—but never aimed in his direction. It had always been the two of them together...going through training, facing battle, taking out bad guys. Either of them could quell the arguments of others with a look. When they walked into a room of civilians, people stared. They'd both been told their confidence was sexy...

Why was Cliff only seeing this side of Ryan now? Was it all drink? That made no sense—they'd been drunk together plenty of times. Seen each other naked a thousand times. Hell—they'd seen each other hard, too. He could recall quite clearly the apartment they'd shared fresh out of BUDs and—and the night Rhino had overlooked the lanyard hanging on Cliff's door and stumbled in to catch sight of Cliff's dick shoved down some guy's throat. Ryan had teased him for weeks before Cliff finally told him guys really knew what another man wanted. The sonofabitch was using his own words against him.

The horny ass had just come off mission and probably needed to get off and didn't care who sucked him. Or was there something more?

For fuck's sake. I can't just stand here all night thinking about it.

Ryan's eyelids were heavy, almost lazy as he blinked up at him, and his mouth curved up on one side, as if he'd been following Cliff's jumbled thoughts. He pressed down once again, and this time, Cliff followed the silent direction and dropped to his knees, ignoring the sexy as sin moan of satisfaction from Ryan when he thought he'd won.

There was nothing subtle about the way he drew the tip of Ryan's cock into his mouth. He wrapped his lips around the fat, leaking tip and got his first salty taste as he sucked hard…almost too hard.

Ryan dragged in a breath, then grabbed Cliff's hair, holding him in place for a long minute. Finally, he placed his palms on Cliff's cheeks and tilted his face, a silent command to look up. When he did, Cliff inhaled sharply at the hungry, almost possessive look.

Ryan's eyes narrowed as he traced his thumbs over Cliff's mouth, his lips stretched around the heavy swollen cock. "That's not the way this is going to go, Cliff. This isn't a race, and nobody's being punished. Show me you want this, baby…"

Fuck. If Ryan called him baby one more time with that little growl in his voice, Cliff might just fucking shoot right here and now.

Closing his eyes in order to break whatever spell Ryan wove over the two of them, Cliff slowly started to move, savoring the taste and feel of Ryan's shaft before pulling off with a wet pop. He buried his face between Ryan's legs, forcing him to widen his stance. He pressed against the coarse hair at Ryan's groin with his fingers, thumbs behind his balls, creating a perfect frame with his hands. Nuzzling in for a moment, he captured the unique smell of Ryan, breathing deeply, memorizing. Drawing his sac forward, Cliff dragged his tongue over the sensitive skin, following the wrinkles and ridges, using the pattern of Ryan's ragged breathing to guide his movements. He pulled one of the orbs gently into his mouth and sucked, enjoying the way Ryan moaned for him. Cliff repeated the process then took the whole sac into his mouth, his cheeks stretched to their limits, tongue separating the fragile balls, massaging, teasing.

Ryan's knees wobbled a little when Cliff released his sac to move back up his cock, laving, stroking.

"That's it...good. So good," Ryan murmured, his voice like black velvet.

A thrill of excitement swirled low in Cliff's belly at Ryan's tone. Nothing in his life could have prepared him for this—the forbidden thrill of taking his best friend in his mouth, making him weak with need. He moved his mouth faster, licking up drops of pre-cum with his own moan of pleasure.

Ryan's big hand wrapped around the back of his neck, pulling him forward, encouraging him to take more, pushing his hips forward in time to Cliff's sucking. His heart thundered uncontrollably as Ryan continued to encourage him with "Yeah, baby" and "So good."

The dialogue would have sounded cheesy in a porn video, but the endearments seemed to go right to Cliff's dick. He worked a hand inside his boxers, stroking himself as he continued to suck and lick Ryan. His gaze traveled up Ryan's hard body, caressing each curve and swell of the chiseled pecs and tight abs. He knew the brutal workouts that put each of those muscles in place. For years they'd worked side by side as they sweated and pushed each other, dragged each other through sand and water. They'd held each other and cried when they'd lost their first teammate. And the second…

They'd stared into each other's eyes, and with no need to speak their thoughts aloud, had shared both agony and exhilaration. Now, he was here, on his knees, and taking his best friend somewhere he'd never been before—and dear lord, don't let it be something that would cost them both.

"Stay right here, Cliff—focus on me," Ryan said. The hand in his hair tightened, then he was held in place as Ryan pushed deeper, cutting off Cliff's breath for half a second—just long enough to let him know who was in control of this blow job.

"Just like that, Cliff. Going to do it again—"

Cliff's throat spasmed around the thick cock as Ryan repeated the move, holding him in place longer, his prick deeper than the last time.

"So good, baby. Don't stop," Ryan ordered.

Wrapping one hand around Ryan's ass, Cliff took him again, pulling Ryan forward, groaning as the fist in his hair tightened, holding him captive until his eyes stung with the need to breathe.

"One more time," Ryan said, only giving Cliff a moment to suck in another breath. He shoved his cock deep, his legs trembling with the effort it took to remain upright, even propped against the wall.

When he released Cliff this time, he could have sworn Ryan whispered, "Good boy," which given he was both older and bigger, made no sense. Bobbing his mouth more quickly now, a raw noise ripped from his throat as Ryan pistoned into his mouth. Cliff's fist flew over his own cock as he dug his fingers into the fleshy globe of Ryan's ass, encouraging him to go faster, pound harder.

The muscles beneath his fingers grew impossibly tight as Ryan lost his rhythm and his breath rushed out in a harsh grunt. Hot cum coated his tongue and spurted down his throat, the first shot all it took to trigger his own release. They finished on gasping moans of mutual pleasure.

"Fuck, yeah," Ryan sighed. He looped his hands under Cliff's pits and dragged him up into a quick, hard kiss. He stroked Cliff's dick through his wet boxers, as if he'd actually intended to do anything about it. When he found evidence of Cliff's release, he gave a light squeeze.

"Hmm...we might need to work on your control next time." There was a hint of laughter in his voice, and Cliff was painfully reminded of just how much Ryan had to drink earlier.

There wasn't a chance in hell his best friend would forget what they'd just done, but there was very little room for doubt how this would play out. This was the beginning of the end of a friendship that meant more than any quick blow job. No fuck was worth the price he'd just paid. Cliff twisted away, mumbled a quick good night, then retreated to his room. The lock made a satisfying click as it turned.

Chapter Six

Given the new ranch duties Cliff had temporarily assumed here at the WSR, Ryan was unsurprised to find himself alone in the casita. What did surprise him was how good he felt despite how much he'd had to drink. Skipping the team R and R in Hawaii meant it was up to him to rebuild his tolerance for alcohol alone. It made him a cheap drunk. He snorted, then moaned as a spike of pain shot through his temples.

Okay, maybe declaring I feel good is a bit premature.

Wincing, he padded into the bathroom, rummaged in the medicine cabinet, and found some ibuprofen. After dry swallowing four, he turned on the shower, adjusted the temperature to one degree below scalding, then stepped under the pounding spray. Ryan stood unmoving for close to five minutes as the water beat against his shoulders and back, his mind filled with nothing but the pleasure of a perfect shower. Hot water was almost always in short supply on a mission.

As he soaped his body, his mind was hit with memories of the night before, of Cliff on his knees...

Those familiar lips in a completely unfamiliar and unexpected position: wrapped around his cock. As if in response to the thoughts, his dick started to fill. He owed Cliff an apology. For nearly twenty years it had been a running joke between them that a man knew how to give a better blow job than any woman. Looked like his old friend was right.

Now just where the hell am I supposed to put that knowledge?

He hurried through the rest of his shower, before he was tempted to jack off to the image of Cliff taking a pounding like he'd never even tried on another person. Did Cliff have any idea how fucking hot he was on his knees, submitting to Ryan?

Blowing out a breath and firmly banishing all thoughts of the previous evening, Ryan stepped from the shower, quickly ran a towel the size of a sheet over his body, before throwing on the uniform of the day: jeans and a T-shirt. He could seriously get used to that.

Once he dressed, he stood in the kitchen, studying the contents of the refrigerator. It was fully stocked, mostly with fruits, vegetables, and salad as far as Ryan could tell without digging.

Where the hell was the bacon? He flicked a glance at the grinder next to the coffee pot and decided he deserved to have someone else care for him in his weakened state. He might not know Ty as well as

Cliff did, but the man was a damned fine cook—and there was sure to be coffee. Maybe there'd be leftover chicken wings from last night's party, too.

Pushing his way outside, Ryan squinted in the bright sunlight. He absently reached for the sunglasses normally hanging from his collar only to remember they were clipped to the sun visor in his Jeep. Circling back around, he retrieved his dark aviator-style glasses and slipped them on. The second Jeep that had been in front of their casita yesterday was gone. *Huh. Where the hell did Cliff go that he needed to drive?* Didn't cowboys ride horses?

His gaze flicked to the three Gator ATVs lined up outside the barn, giving lie to that stereotype. Remembering at the last second to not shake his head and disturb the fragile well-being attained in the shower, Ryan headed for the main house.

As he walked across the hard-packed dirt, he slowed his steps while he debated the merits of a front door versus back door just-dropping-in visit. Since he was clearly intent on food and coffee, it seemed the kitchen was the easier target. Just as he veered in that direction, the door swung inward and Ty waved him over.

The man stood in the door in stocking feet, worn blue jeans, and a T-shirt...obviously he'd gotten the same memo about the uniforms.

"You look like shit," he said as Ryan made his way inside.

"Yeah, thanks. Feel like it too. Any chance of some coffee? And I don't suppose you could whip up a couple of one-eyed jacks?"

Ty laughed. "Don't suppose, huh?" He pointed to the bench just inside the door. "Put your shoes there, then come on in. We'll see what we can find."

While Ryan sat to remove his boots, Ty headed into the kitchen, followed by the sound of clanging pots. Ryan sauntered inside and took a good look around the industrialized home kitchen. The counters were all business stainless steel, the appliances restaurant grade, the organization and cleanliness totally Ty's Navy background.

"Grab yourself a cup of coffee. The urn in the dining room has standard grade, this pot here"—he pointed to a small coffee maker on the counter—"will put hair on your chest."

Ryan stretched the collar of his shirt and peered down at his chest. "Too late," he mumbled. He crossed to the kitchen pot and poured the thick hot brew into his cup, then blew impatiently across the surface before cautiously taking the first sip.

"Ahhhh," he moaned. "I might just live to fight another day."

Ty's mouth quirked up on one side. "One of the best things about returning from a mission," he said, his voice laced with laughter. "That and a…"

Their gazes met at the old joke. "Shower," they finished in unison.

"Give me a couple of minutes…" Ty strode to the freezer and removed three frozen hamburger patties. They sizzled when he dropped them on the hot grill before he returned to the refrigerator for three eggs. "Cheese?"

"Oh god, yes please," Ryan said with a little whimper for effect.

Ten minutes later, Ty put a plate in front of him with three sliders, each burger topped with a fried egg and a thick slice of cheese. Ryan squeezed some ketchup onto his plate, used it to dip the edge of the bun before taking his first bite. His eyes closed in ecstasy. "Ohmyfgdn," he mumbled around the mouthful of food.

Ty refilled their coffee cups then leaned against the counter to watch Ryan wolf down his burgers.

When Ryan had cleaned his plate and tossed down the napkin in a show of victory over the monstrous pile of food, he looked up at Ty. "Thanks, man. That might have been the best I've had to eat…well, other than last night—but I can't tell you the last time I had a one-eyed jack."

"Haven't made 'em since I was in…" He took a swallow of coffee as his gaze drifted to the kitchen window. "Afghanistan," he finished softly.

"Yeah…fucking sucks," Ryan said. He pushed to his feet and brought his plate around to the sink, but in truth, Ty's comments set off a chain reaction of feelings too big to hold while sitting in one place. Ty had received a medical discharge after sustaining injuries…but his reputation among the SEALs he'd served with was solid. The dude was a stone cold killer who could cook.

"Did you feel pushed out too soon?" Ryan blurted, thinking of Cliff and the lack of choice his friend felt.

Leveling his blue-eyed gaze at Ryan, Ty nodded. "Yeah, definitely." Then following Ryan's train of thought, he added, "It's not the same for Cliff, though."

"Why, because he's older than you?"

"That might be part of it," Ty conceded. "But honestly, this shore duty assignment was killing him—and he's been restless for a couple of years. Just because he doesn't exactly know what he wants to do next, doesn't mean he isn't ready to move on."

The words seemed to itch inside Ryan's brain. Maybe because he hadn't known Cliff felt restless…then again, they hadn't been around each other as much over the last two years due to their different duty assignments. They both were still stationed in Coronado, but serving on different teams made their regular off duty time more difficult to schedule. Or maybe the itch was because they so closely echoed his own thoughts about his current situation.

"I got offered Six," he confided.

Ty straightened. "Yeah? Did you already pass the board?" Ty asked, referring to the intensive screening every candidate endured as part of the assignment process before starting training for the DEVGRU.

"Nah...haven't given them an answer yet. I have..." He looked at his Luminox dive watch. "Seventy-two more hours before I need to tell the old man."

"Gonna take it?"

"I don't know. I suppose it sorta depends on Snides..."

"What do you mean?"

"I'm thinking about asking the skipper to reconsider his decision to have Cliff retire. Obviously there's a need for shooters on Six, and Snides and I are one of the best two-man strike teams around. If I could—"

Ty was shaking his head. "You know that's not possible, Ryan. He told you what happened—right?"

"Yeah, but—"

"Look, Cliff is more ready to retire than you think he is—but just say he did stay in, nobody's going to put the two of you together on any mission."

"What the fuck? Why would you say that?" Ryan's temper spiked. Ty didn't even know him, not really. What the hell did Ty know about how he and Cliff worked together?

Ty blinked at him, and suddenly Ryan felt like he was under a microscope. After a long moment of study, Ty sighed. "You're too emotionally attached, Rhino."

"Emotionally attached?"

"Okay, call it love, then. If I were in charge of a mission and the two of you were on my team, I'd avoid putting you in harm's way together because your judgment might be impaired by a need to protect Cliff—and vice versa."

"What the— *Love?*" Rather than repeat the WTF words, Ryan took a different tack. "We're brothers—like any team members would be—but mission always comes first."

Shaking his head, Ty disagreed. "Maybe once…not anymore. How long's it been since the two of you were assigned together?"

"Five years, but—"

"I bet command was talking about it even then…probably assumed you were lovers on the down low from DADT before it got rescinded."

Ryan started to laugh. He couldn't help it. "Shit, Ty...people have been talking about us for ages." His smile remained in place as he thought of Mad Max calling them an old married couple.

"There's a major problem with that theory. I'm straight. Hell, I even have an ex-wife to prove it." He grinned and shook his head at how off base Ty was.

"I didn't know you were married—that doesn't work out for a lot of special forces..." Ty said. "Were you and Cliff friends then?"

"Sure. It wasn't long after BUDs training."

"How'd your ex feel about Cliff?"

Ryan snorted. "She was jealous as hell of all the time we spent—" He shook his head. "Oh no—nice try, cook boy. That is not why we got divorced and it wasn't that kind of jealousy. I was too young and stupid to know better. I was just looking for someplace... Something..." He stopped sputtering for a minute, wondering if he even knew what he'd been looking for all those years ago.

"You're twisting my words, Ty. I'm not gay," he said quietly.

"Does the label matter? Look..." Ty paused and stared at his coffee cup for a long moment, then looked at Ryan. "I've known I was gay my whole life, but hid it for a variety of reasons...but being gay didn't stop me from having sex with women. I'm sure you've heard of the Kinsey Scale. Sure some people are only drawn to partners of the same sex. Others are completely heterosexual. But most people fall somewhere between the two extremes."

Ty turned away to retrieve the glass carafe, filled both cups with coffee, then continued. "My point— which seems to be taking a long time to make— maybe you're not gay or straight, but bisexual. There's nothing to say you aren't genuinely attracted to women, but that doesn't mean you can't be attracted to—or fall in love with—a man. With Cliff."

"You think I'm in love with Cliff?" Ryan asked and wondered if Ty noticed the breathy quality of his voice. Surely that was just because of the odd misconception Ty had. Wasn't it?

Ty shrugged his big shoulders. "I don't know…maybe. I'd say you spend an unusual amount of time preoccupied with thoughts of him, for someone you claim is just a friend. Even a best friend. You were certainly pretty close to a panic by the time you tracked Cliff here. And you'd been CONUS— what? All of twenty-four hours?"

Ryan caught himself about to nod, then shook his head instead. "I don't see myself that way…"

"That way? What way is that? Some preconceived notion of how a gay man is supposed to act? Let me tell you what I saw last night. I saw two men who obviously care a great deal about each other. The two of you were joined at the hip, clearly happy to be reunited after your tour of duty. Neither of you hesitated to touch the other on the arm, the back, the thigh…and your gaze was glued to his backside whenever he walked across the room. You brought each other food and drinks without needing to ask what the other wanted—hell, you finished each other's sentences half the time and had the silent conversation thingy going on with your eyes. You two acted like more of a couple than many of the couples in the room."

"We've been told that before," Ryan admitted.

Ty laughed. "No doubt. The thing is, you're more free with the touching than he is. Cliff is…careful. I imagine he's gotten used to remaining hands off—a lot of gay men in the military are that way. It keeps things a lot less complicated when you don't send mixed signals. Hell, you'd probably have to make a pretty big first move—like maybe a two-by-four over the head—just to convince him you're serious."

"But I don't—" He rubbed his chin, trying to figure where the hell he'd been going with that thought. Listening to Ty's rapid delivery observations and taking it all in was like trying to swallow water from a fire hose. He was spilling a lot more than he could absorb at this moment.

"It's something to think about," Ty said with a shrug. "I guess I'd tell you not to take too long, though. You need to let the Navy know what you're going to do—and Cliff needs to move forward with the rest of his life. With or without you."

"What's that supposed to mean…and where is Cliff this morning, anyway?"

Shaking his head, Ty clicked his tongue against his teeth. "Don't you tell each other anything? What the hell did you do last night after the Super Bowl?"

With a casual shrug of his shoulder, Ryan leaned back and curved his mouth up on one side. There was no way he'd tell Ty what he and Cliff had done last night. He still hadn't decided how he felt about it, and now, given Ty's assertion that he and Cliff had feelings beyond friendship…

"Didn't do a thing except crash. I was pretty wiped after the travel and the margaritas. Why?"

"Oh man…you might be trained to withstand hours of enemy interrogation, but you're shitty at evading someone who has a pretty good idea of the truth."

Frowning, Ryan raised his cup and sipped his coffee. "I'm not sure what you're talking about. Listen, I've got to get back. Where did you say Cliff was working today?"

Laughter spilled out and Ty had a hard time getting his words out between chuckles. "Cliff went back to San Diego—"

Ryan straightened and set his cup on the counter with a thunk. "What the—"

"Chill. He had to meet the detective on the shooting case this morning and tomorrow he's finishing his retirement paperwork. He'll be back by dinnertime tomorrow night. It's a funny thing, but Cliff had almost the same reaction as you when I asked him what you two did last night." Ty walked to the refrigerator and removed packets of lunchmeat and a couple of storage containers and tossed them onto the counter then retrieved a cardboard box from the walk-in pantry. He started filling the box with what looked to be a very promising assortment of goodies. "I'm not going to stick my nose in where it doesn't belong—"

Ryan snorted. "Too fucking late for that. Honestly, Ty, I appreciate what you're saying, I just don't know if I can…well, you've given me a shitload to think about."

"Here, take this," he said, sliding it across the counter toward Ryan. "Cliff has all that health food crap in the fridge. I figure you can use real nourishment. Of course you're welcome here any time. As far as what to do about Cliff?" Ty grinned. "Google free gay porn—you'll figure it out."

Chapter Seven

"Master Chief Snyder? I'm Kam Wagner. Nice to meet you. Thanks for agreeing to look at more photos," the man said, flashing an ID card and a bright smile as they briefly shook hands. Kam gestured for Cliff to follow him through the electronically secured door, and they walked along the fluorescent-lighted bowels of the thirty-year-old San Diego Police Headquarters building.

Kam moved with quiet confidence, his strides long, each step rolling him up on his toes so he almost bounced as they passed through the long hallway. When they entered an open bullpen of desks and detectives, several pairs of eyes followed their progress. He exchanged a look with Detective Kingston—the man who'd interviewed him on his previous visit to the SDPD. The detective's mouth twisted into a mockery of a smile as he glanced from Cliff to Kam and back again. *Huh. Wonder what that's about?*

Ignoring the looks, Kam led the way to one of several glass-fronted offices that lined the back wall and gestured unsmilingly for Cliff to step inside. The impersonal space was a step up from the interrogation room with the two-way glass where Kingston had taken him to look at the mug books shortly after the shootings.

Closing the door, probably to give a small illusion of privacy, Kam looked up at Cliff. "Sorry about that. Nothing like taking you through a parade of gawkers to put you at your ease, huh?"

Wagner's voice held a hint of sarcasm, and he figured this was the round of good cop, since Kingston's homophobic attitude had clearly put him on the side of bad cop—and not in a good way.

Several notebooks were stacked on one end of the oval conference table, so without waiting to be asked, Cliff squeezed his way around Kam and rested his hand on the tall-back office chair. He gazed out through the windows at the sea of desks, catching more curious gazes. After a moment he turned to study Detective Wagner. Probably standing at five-ten in his boots, the man's face was smooth, unlined, with no trace of a beard. His dark brown hair was worn long, the loose curls just touching his shoulders. The sleeves of his olive green Henley were pushed up to reveal smooth forearms, his jeans were worn long enough to fray where they caught on the heel of his heavy boots.

"Jesus," Cliff blurted. "Are you even old enough to drink?"

"My mommy even let me stay up to watch the game with all the grown-ups last night," Kam said. His grin said he appreciated rather than resented the comment. "I'm blessed with some good genes. This"—he pointed to his face—"allowed me to work undercover with youth gangs a helluva long time. I'm just a little too long in the tooth for that now, but I don't mind. It gets pretty fucking old hanging out with a bunch of delinquent teenagers."

"Gangs, huh? Someone is finally admitting it's a gang-involved crime now? I tried to tell that to Kingston last week."

"Have a seat, Master Chief," Kam invited as he moved around the table to take a chair next to Cliff, so they could both sit with their backs to a wall.

"Call me Cliff. No need for titles. I'm on terminal leave, waiting until my retirement becomes official at the end of the month."

Kam's eyes narrowed and he looked Cliff full in the face. The younger man's scrutiny made him hyper-aware of how he must look. With his salt-and-pepper hair, two-day beard, and bags under his eyes the size of plums from too little sleep followed by a five-hour drive, he probably looked a decade older than his forty years.

"I'll call you by your name if you like, but my dad retired from the Navy, and taught me a lot about respect. As he used to say before he passed, once a chief, always a chief. You made it to the top of the enlisted ranks, and as one of the elite, so don't let this"—his gaze dropped to the books, then swept the outer office where most of the detectives had gone back to minding their own duties—"single incident diminish your accomplishments."

Definitely the good cop.

"You didn't answer my question," Cliff said, rather than responding to the pep-talk, as he sat and rested his forearms on the table. "So it's confirmed? The shooting and robbery were gang-related?"

"That's the working theory. Look, let's get this out of the way first. I'm familiar with the reports, I saw the crime scene photos, I know what Hard Labour was, and I don't give a shit. Can we be clear on that, before we do anything else?"

"If you say so. Where do you want me to start?"

With an ill-disguised snort of amusement, Kam pointed to the book on the top. For the next thirty minutes, neither of them spoke as Cliff dutifully scanned each page of photos. The assortment of photos differed from the mug books Detective Kingston showed him the day following the shootings. Those had been younger men and many of the faces black. These books were primarily Hispanic, the men ranging in age from late teens to mid-thirties. Which was closer to the age he'd estimated the older man to be.

On the bottom corner of the third page of his third book, he found a face that looked familiar. Mentally noting the location, he decided to finish the book, then return to the photo.

"Spot something?" Kam asked. The man was a good observer.

"Maybe." He tapped his finger on the photo and turned the book toward Wagner. "This one looks…similar. Like your buddy over there pointed out"—he tilted his head in Kingston's direction—"I wasn't in a position to have an unobstructed view. It's never going to be enough to hold up in court—"

Detective Wagner's face went blank as he stared through the office window. David Kingston leaned a hip against his desk, his gaze on the two of them, his mouth running to the apparent amusement of the two men standing next to him.

Finally, Kam dragged his attention back to Cliff. "Detective Kingston's not working this case anymore, I am. As for testifying? That's too far down the road for either of us to worry about. Right now, we just want to find that first thread…the one loose end that will unravel the whole case. Know what I mean?"

"Yeah, I know. I wish I could tell you this"—he tapped the photo—"is it, but I don't think so. The first man…the older one who was shouting orders…" He blew out a breath as just for a moment he relived the frustration of remaining handcuffed to a bed while Draco and Gentry were shot down less than twenty feet away. "This could be a relative of the older man. The face structure is similar, but this man is six-one according to the mug shot…the shooter was five-ten, tops."

"All right, do me a favor. Shake your head, close that book, and take the last one. Go ahead and look through all the photos, just like you've been doing. If you see someone you recognize, make a note. If you don't see any familiar faces, let's talk over another photo anyway."

Cliff was far too disciplined to visibly react to Kam's words, but he understood the implication well enough. Kingston, or someone else Kam had seen when he'd stared out at the bullpen just now tweaked the detective's radar. He clearly didn't want it known if Cliff made an ID.

An hour later, Cliff sat sipping from a large black coffee to-go from Cozy's and watched Kam Wagner dodge cars as he crossed the street to join him.

"Isn't that called jaywalking?" he teased lightly.

"That's why I was running," Kam said, a smile flittering over his handsome face for an instant.

Already intrigued by the request to depart as normal, then circle around to move his Jeep from the street parking spot in front of the PD to a parking structure a few blocks away, his curiosity spiked further as Kam hustled him around the corner. They headed toward the back entrance of a single story brick building that might have housed a grocery store in the forties and fifties. The structure had been modified with a wide portico and double automated doors marked Emergency Personnel Only. New Horizons was painted onto the old brick wall to the left side of the door.

The smell of disinfectant assaulted him as they came through the entrance. A single man in teal scrubs half-rose from the rolling chair behind the desk at the nurse's station, his lips parted as if to say something. Kam held up his badge and kept moving, and the nurse fell back into his seat with a little wave. Obviously the detective was both recognized and knew exactly where he was headed.

The interior was laid out like a ladder, with two long corridors running front to back and shorter connecting hallways running side to side. They passed several open doors, each revealing a standard hospital room, complete with two beds, curtains hanging from the ceiling, and patients staring at wall-mounted televisions. Taking a right turn, nothing changed much except the door at the end was closed and clearly marked a *Do Not Enter* zone. Numerous Day-Glo orange signed screamed this room contained an infectious patient. The two rooms on either side appeared empty, probably to reduce any risk of contamination.

"Detective Wagner," he said after rapping twice on the door. Without waiting for an invitation, he pushed on the handle and stepped inside.

With more than a passing suspicion things were not what they seemed and completely drawn into the cloak-and-dagger atmosphere the detective created, Cliff followed him through the door.

"About time you fucking got here."

The man on the bed was a shell of the man he'd met with the previous week. Draco Kincaid. A very much alive Draco Kincaid. Although from the array of machines surrounding the bed, it looked like it might have been touch and go for a while.

"Nicely played Detective Wagner," Cliff said.

"Take a break," Wagner said to the fresh-faced plainclothes officer who had been seated just inside the door to the room.

As Cliff moved around the bed to an angle that allowed Draco to look at him without fighting the immobilizing neck brace or head restraints, Kam moved to stand next to the opposite side of the bed.

"That's close enough," Wagner barked. Cliff glanced up and saw the detective was on full alert, as if he expected Cliff to make some sort of move against the club owner.

"Get a grip, Wagner," Draco said, his gaze flicking toward the right, then back left toward Cliff. "I told you Cliff was an innocent bystander."

"You also told me you don't remember anything about the attack and you have no idea what anyone could have been looking for—pardon me if I call bullshit. Let's cut to the chase. I got Kingston off the case. I brought Snyder here and kept it off the record—just like you requested. Now it's time to tell me what's going on."

Draco's gaze fixed on Cliff's, the plea obvious—but that didn't mean Cliff had a clue what the other man needed. Asking questions of his own might give them all a few minutes to regroup.

"I can see maybe there was a reason the cops on scene kept me in the back, so the EMTs could get you out. What about Gentry?"

"He didn't stand a chance. The sons a bitches nearly cut him in half," Draco said. "And for the record...I still don't know why the fuck they chose Hard Labour. You tell me they mentioned a disk, Kam, but I just don't have those memories. I'm stuck in this fucking bed without even a clear look at the television to distract me. Don't you think I've replayed the scene a million times already?"

"So what disk, Draco? Even if you don't remember what they said, tell me what was on it. Membership data? Why the fuck would anyone care?"

Draco gave a humorless laugh that turned into a cough. By the time he caught his breath his eyes had gone glassy. "No one should care, but people would.

We've had more than a few people considered celebrities visit on occasion. But, Kam, you gotta believe me, I just didn't have a disk like that. I give you my word this doesn't have anything to do with our few remaining members. I told you I was phasing that out—my club was closing."

"Then tell me what it does have to do with and what was on the disk."

"If they took the disk I kept in the safe, then they'll be pretty fucking unhappy, because it's a copy of my tax filings from my accountant. I've told you the name of every person I can remember, but I was getting ready to sell the building and shut the club down—there was no reason to hang on to old data. Sorry, Kam, I know that's not what you want to hear, but it's all you're going to get."

"Then why the fuck did you tell me to bring Cliff here? You said you'd tell me everything if I got Cliff."

Draco's face relaxed infinitesimally, as if he was carefully wiping away any lingering clues to his thoughts. Which meant whatever came next would probably be a lie. "I thought maybe if I saw the last person I spoke with, maybe more memories would come back—but there's just nothing there, Kam. Not one fucking thing—" He stopped speaking, his mouth hanging open for half a second.

"What is it? Did you think of something else?"

Draco's eyes canted right as he strained to make eye contact with Wagner. "The money?"

"The operating cash," the detective prompted. He moved closer to the bed, practically hovering over Kincaid's prone body. "You said there would have been seventy-five hundred in operating cash for the next day's till. Not paltry, but it seems a little low for robbery-homicide."

"Yes," Draco's voice was fading, and each word seemed an effort. His complexion had faded from pale to gray and his eyelids drooped. "Not that. Kept cash. Hundred. Grand." He drew in a raspy breath.

A knock at the door stopped the conversation. Without waiting for an invitation to enter, a Hispanic woman dressed in SpongeBob SquarePants scrubs pushed her way inside, followed closely by the man who'd been guarding Draco when they'd arrived.

"That's enough for today, Detective," the nurse said as she assumed Kam's spot at the head of the bed. She placed a tray with two syringes on the rolling table and started making adjustments to the IV, obviously preparing to administer some pain relief.

Leaving Wagner to follow the movements of the nurse, Cliff watched Draco's face. Their gazes locked briefly before the other man closed his lids, his mouth pinched at the corner before turning down into a frown.

"Hang on, Nurse. A hundred K?" Kam asked, his voice rising in obvious surprise.

"Yes. In bundled hundreds."

"Jesus. Why the fuck didn't you say so…"

"Out," the nurse ordered.

"Wait a second, Becky," Draco half moaned. "Cliff, need a favor. When the cops are done with my place—need you to close up shop. Post signs. Get cleaning service—"

"Don't worry about a thing, Draco. I happen to have some free time on my hands."

"Stay there if you want—apartment's upstairs."

"Enough, already," the nurse said, nailing them all with a say-one-more-word-and-you-die look.

Not often one to miss the obvious, Cliff didn't give anyone a chance to stop him, just leaned down to give Draco a good-bye hug, managing to place his ear over the other man's mouth and used his forearms to shield them from prying eyes.

The whisper was soft, but clear. "When Rhino gets CONUS…need him."

A few minutes later they were pushing their way out the back door into the bright afternoon sunlight of a perfect San Diego afternoon. Only the day didn't taste quite as good as it should have.

"What's wrong with him? What's the prognosis?" he asked Kam.

"There's a bullet lodged near his spine. The doctors gave him no chance for survival when they brought him in. I understand they've revised their estimate after he regained consciousness and chewed all their asses."

Cliff snorted. "Is he gonna walk again?"

"Doubtful. He's not out of the woods yet. I hear they may need to do surgery again once the swelling goes down. They don't know if they'll be able to remove the bullet or stabilize it, but the damage to his spinal column is devastating. If he survives, the main question is whether he'll be a para or quadriplegic."

"Fuck."

"Exactly. So now, you want to tell me why he wants you to go to his place?"

"I have no fucking clue. I mean other than the obvious."

"Obvious?"

"Yeah. You have him in isolation—I'm assuming I'm the only person who knows he's still alive?"

Kam jerked his head in agreement.

"Okay, so his business is basically done, but given its location in the old warehouse district, that building has got to be worth a hell of a lot of money these days…"

"Millions," Kam agreed.

"So all he really wants is someone taking care of his investment until he's able to do it himself. I assume you know the man is a former SEAL…"

"I do my homework."

"Then you know we're all brothers. Draco and I might not know each other well, but he's in trouble…and he'd know, without being told, what it cost me to get caught in his club"—Cliff gazed back at the rehab center—"under those circumstances while thugs committed murder in the other room. This is probably his way of making things better for both of us."

"I'll let you know when you're cleared to enter the club. It should be another couple of days. Then I think maybe you and I should see if anyone is watching…"

"Gonna make me a target, Wagner?"

"If I have to. Unless you want to tell me what Draco…and now you…are hiding…"

"Looking forward to it," Cliff said. Then, humming the theme song to the Roadrunner cartoon, he sauntered away.

Chapter Eight

Ryan glanced at the clock for the third time in fifteen minutes and wondered where in the hell Cliff was. Then he wondered what in the hell he was doing. Damn Tyler Hardin for putting ideas in his head anyway.

Moving to the kitchen, Ryan turned the oven down to warm, per Ty's directions, assured even if nothing else about this night went as planned, at least the roasted chicken and potato casserole would come out right. The table was set, the sheets were clean, and the nightstands stocked with plenty of lube and even condoms if Cliff deemed them necessary. And…if everything went tits up, there was a whole season of *Sons of Anarchy* on Netflix to look forward to.

Just the thought of sinking into Cliff's tight ass had Ryan's cock filling. *Jesus.* It wasn't like he hadn't jacked off half a dozen times the last two days. Who knew there was so much free gay porn on the Internet?

The familiar growl of an engine drew his gaze to the window just as headlights flickered against the glass. Unease mingled with excitement as Ryan once again weighed his options. Grab Cliff by the shirtfront and kiss the shit out of him the minute he walked through the door...or dinner and talk, then kiss him? For someone trained to improvise under life or death circumstances, this dilemma was kicking his ass.

"Hey," Cliff said, stepping through the door. Although his tone was casual, the tightness of his square jaw spoke volumes about his best friend's level of tension. Hell, Cliff had probably spent the whole return trip from San Diego worrying how Ryan would greet him after the other night. If only he knew...

"Smells good in here. Did you cook dinner?" Cliff asked as he crossed to his bedroom door and tossed his overnight bag inside.

Deciding to go with the flow, Ryan nodded. "Sort of. Ty gave me a head start. All I had to do was stick it in the oven. He said you went to San Diego..." *Awkward much?*

Cliff looked down at him for a long moment, his steel gray eyes narrowed, the lines fanning away from his normal smiling expression. "Yeah...uh, Rhino? Are we okay? Did I fuck things up between us the other night?"

That was his Cliff—never met a problem he wouldn't tackle head on. He smiled and stepped closer. "It didn't mess anything up for me, Snides. How about for you? You left pretty quick yesterday morning…"

He placed a hand on Cliff's heavily muscled forearm.

"Uh…yeah. I had a meeting set up with the new detective assigned to the case. We didn't exactly get around to talking about that with the Super Bowl and—"

Ryan traced his fingers over Cliff's bicep, the heated skin sending shots of electricity through his fingertips. "Go on…"

"I…uhm…" Cliff's gaze lingered on Ryan's fingers. "My uh…paperwork. Had to finish—Ryan?" Their gazes locked. Cliff's eyes widened and his tongue skated over his lower lip.

Intentional or not, Ryan took the gesture as an invitation and closed the distance between them. He slid his hand along Cliff's shoulder to cup the back of the taller man's neck, then applied a not-so-subtle pressure. Leaning into the move, he closed the final distance separating them and captured Cliff's mouth in a kiss. For half a second, he thought it might be that easy. Lips parted on a sigh, tongues touched, and they melted against each other. Almost immediately though, Cliff stiffened and jerked back.

"What are you doing?"

"I thought it was obvious. It's called kissing."

"Yes, I know what it's called. What I don't get is why—" Cliff yanked his arm back from Ryan's loose grip. "Give me a fucking break, Ryan. That was a one-time event. I never should have done it and I sure as hell don't plan to be on permanent BJ duty until you get back to Coronado and find a woman to fuck."

"So *not* what I'm thinking, Cliff. I should have…" Ryan shook his head. "Shit. We should have talked first, I guess."

"Ya think? What's this about, Ryan?"

Needing a few minutes to get his thoughts together, Ryan turned away and walked toward the kitchen. "Want a beer?" he asked as he opened the fridge and removed a bottle of sparkling water for himself.

"Do I need one? No—don't answer that. I'll have what you're having. Now, will you please explain?"

"Yeah…I think I will." Ryan twisted the top from a bottle and placed it on the counter for Cliff, before opening his own bottle. He took a long drink before starting his explanation. As well as they knew each other, this just wasn't a conversation he'd ever expected to have. It was why he'd changed his mind about how to proceed half a dozen times over the last two days.

However, they were long past the go-no-go decision point. He'd committed to action when he'd kissed Cliff, so now it was time to follow through. "I had breakfast and a long talk with Ty yesterday. He had some interesting observations about how the two of us act around each other. He forced me to look at some assumptions I'd always made. Cliff, you know how people have teased us for years about acting like a married couple?"

Cliff was shaking his head...not as if he didn't know, but as if he could deny what Ryan was about to say. "You're straight, Rhino. That doesn't just change overnight. We're friends. Best friends—"

Ryan smiled. "Yeah, we are and have been for twenty years. We've shared more than most couples and maybe people have been seeing something we didn't—we couldn't—because we've always defined the difference between us as gay and straight."

"That's because we are. Rhino...you don't just turn gay because you got your rocks off when another guy sucks you off."

"I don't think I *am* gay. How I feel about women—in the generic sense—hasn't changed. But how I feel about you—or rather how I feel about our relationship—*has* changed."

Cliff sucked in a big breath and let it loose on an explosive bark of laughter. "I told you..." He chuckled some more. "Guys give the best blow jobs—

but Rhino—just teach your next girlfriend how you like it." He continued to laugh. "Seriously…we're good, okay? Let's just forget about this. We can have dinner and watch TV or something."

Setting his bottle on the counter with a thunk, Ryan stalked toward Cliff until he was in his space. He unzipped his pants and tugged Cliff's hand until it rested inside his underwear. The big hand wrapped around Ryan's cock as Cliff studied his face.

"Can't deny this, Cliff. That's for you." He unbuckled the belt on Cliff's slacks, then worked the button and zipper free. Sliding his hands to Cliff's hips, he slipped the fabric down, then dropped to his knees, as if in supplication.

"Waited two days to kiss you, Cliff. Want to touch you." He brushed his cheek against the velvet-soft skin of Cliff's dick. Heat surged through him, searing his soul with an absolute certainty that this was right.

"Want to taste you." He slicked his tongue over the broad tip, capturing the essence of the man he was sure he loved. The salty bitter flavor burst on his tongue and saliva pooled in his mouth. He swallowed rapidly, trying to keep from drooling, and Cliff inhaled sharply.

Putting his hands on Ryan's shoulders, Cliff made a half-hearted attempt to pull him off. "Don't need to do this, Ry…"

Closing his eyes, Ryan pictured all the blow jobs he'd watched over the last several hours and concentrated on controlling his gag reflex as he experimented with his favorite bits. Circling his mouth around the tip, a light suction, then a harder pull that elicited a moan from Cliff.

His own answering grin broke the suction so he flicked his tongue out and licked the length like it was his new favorite flavor of ice cream. Tracing over bumps and ridges, he followed a trail back toward the tip. After moistening his lips, Ryan slipped the head of Cliff's cock back in his mouth and started to bob, in and out, up and down. Hot. Wet. Slick.

A hand slid into Ryan's hair, and for a moment, he thought Cliff would force him to take more. Then the fingers tightened and drew him back, halting his movements. Ryan tilted his face up, admiring the perfectly defined abs and pecs. He could hardly wait to taste them. He lingered on Cliff's mouth, remembering the wicked tongue, the hot, willing throat that held him deep. When he finally dragged his gaze all the way up to settle on his friend's face, Cliff's normally light eyes were dark, heavy-lidded…sexy.

"Ryan," Cliff ground out.

"Yeah, baby, it's me. You think we've enough for now? Can we take this to the bedroom?"

"Are you sure? It's not the same… I don't want…"

It might have been crazy, but seeing Cliff's protectiveness mingled with uncertainty twisted Ryan's heart even more. He knew exactly what Cliff was thinking. He worried Ryan didn't realize how profoundly this would change things between them...but he did.

Maybe even more than Cliff did, because Ryan had come to understand something about his friend in the two days since their impromptu Super Bowl celebration. Regardless of why he'd gone to Hard Labour the night of the shooting, Cliff Snyder was no Dom, and a small petty part of his soul hated thinking that, but for fate, Draco Kincaid might have explored that with him first.

"You know I've seen men fucking before—we've been to clubs together, but at Ty's suggestion, I've spent the last two days watching gay porn. Nothing I've seen comes close to all the things I want to do with you. No one else, Cliff. I want you. Want this." He slid his hands over the smooth skin of Cliff's ass, then squeezed the taut cheeks.

That seemed to be what Cliff was waiting for. He tugged at Ryan's shoulders and he rose slowly, his jeans dragging up the length of Cliff's naked thighs.

"Come on, baby. Let me take you to bed," Ryan whispered against Cliff's mouth.

As he took Cliff's hand and led him down the short hall and into the master bedroom, his heart thundered like a runaway train, headed for the abyss. And now he was certain he wouldn't fall alone.

*

Cliff allowed Ryan to drag him toward his bedroom, feeling as if he was caught halfway between a nightmare and a wet dream. With a mental pinch, he reminded himself this was Ryan. Rhino. His best friend. His strike mission partner. Not someone he fucked around with—at least not in the literal sense.

As soon as he neared the bed, Ryan turned. "Finish undressing."

Cliff slowly unbuttoned his dress shirt, watching as Ryan shucked his jeans and pulled his T-shirt over his head. Ryan's erection was thick and long, and pointing straight at Cliff, as if offering proof positive of his desire.

Cliff's fingers fumbled at the last button when Ryan wrapped his hand around his cock and began to stroke himself. Shit, the sight already had Cliff's balls tingling.

Cliff closed the distance between them, drawing Ryan into his arms, needing to feel the solid body, skin touching skin, pushing away any sense of dream. They touched from thigh to chest, shafts mashed together, impossible to ignore.

"If you're going to back away, this would be the time, Rhino," Cliff whispered, even as he wrapped his big hand around both their cocks and began to stroke.

"Not going anywhere, Cliff. Lie back on the bed…let me explore?"

"Timber…" he said, falling back on the mattress. Crawling backward until he was in the center, he added, "Lube is in my shaving kit in the bathroom."

"Some super spy you are," Ryan said with a laugh as he opened the bedside drawer and drew out a bottle and a foil packet. Cliff's stomach clenched. Ryan was going to agree to being fucked? Holy shit. Maybe he should let Ryan finish that blow job just to take the edge off. It wouldn't do to shoot his load on initial penetration.

"I can't wait to bury myself in you," Ryan said, sending Cliff's libido into the stratosphere. "Do we need to use condoms? I've been on a mission since my last HIV test. Completely clean. What about you?"

"I'm clean—but Jesus, Rhino—don't you think—" Cliff shook his head, trying to mash together all of the thoughts into one coherent sentence. Ryan wanted to fuck *him*…somehow that was even hotter. And bareback? Oh holy fuck.

"Cliff…baby. Stop thinking so hard. I can hear the wheels grinding. He tossed the supplies onto the mattress and climbed on the bed, crawling forward until he straddled Cliff's hips. Trailing his fingers over

112

Cliff's stomach, causing his muscles to quiver and jump under the touch, Ryan smiled down at him. "I'm not moving too fast, Cliff. I— I know that's what you're worried about."

"But what if you hate it? Shit, Ry. I'm a gay man—believe me when I tell you your ass is dangerously close to becoming an acquired target right now. I'm so hard I could pound nails...but fuck. We've been friends for twenty years. Are you seriously saying if we do this and you abso-fucking-lutely hate it, that it won't bleed over into everything else. Because I've lost a hell of a lot in the last couple weeks, but nothing that means more than this." He waggled his thumb and index finger between them.

Ryan's mouth curved the slightest bit on an exhale, and the tightness around his eyes softened. He nodded then, as if in response to something he could only hear in his head.

Cliff waited. Ryan never had a thought he wasn't positive Cliff wanted to hear. Most of the time he was right.

"When's the last time you had a date? Not a hookup, but a real date that had you hoping to see the guy again?"

Cliff laughed, but it came out bitter. "Hell if I know. Years. That's something you can't understand, Rhino. A gay man in the Navy—and I don't give a shit what they say about DADT—just isn't going to go around with visions of a second or third date."

"I call bullshit," Ryan said. His fingers began to play with Cliff's chest hair, which made it hard to focus on his words. "More than half the SEALs we know are single...not just you because you're gay. It's hard to maintain a relationship when you're dark for six months on a mission... It's harder when you can't talk about what you do—or you're worried that if your girlfriend found out, she'd hate that essential part of you. There's nothing different about being gay or straight there. Most men assigned to special warfare suck at relationships. Those few who manage to find someone special and maintain a marriage over the course of a career are pretty damned rare."

Closing his eyes, Cliff could think of maybe a dozen happily married long-term couples he'd known over the years. Ryan was right, healthy, normal relations and SEAL were often mutually exclusive.

"Hey, pay attention," Ryan said, giving a sharp tweak to one of Cliff's nipples.

"Owww..."

"You're the one who wanted to talk. So hear me out, oh mighty wise-gay man. In your far more experienced opinion...did I enjoy the blow job you gave me the other night?"

"If I had tonsils, you'd have punched them inside out."

Ryan smiled and flicked Cliff's other nipple, causing his hips to buck and rubbing their cocks together. They both groaned at the contact.

"Point, Rhino?" Cliff asked through clenched teeth.

"Okay, smartass. So try this on for size. Maybe we're like one of those couples. Everyone comments on it. We've been together for twenty goddamn years and neither of us has found someone else we'd rather spend time with—"

"Well, there's an endorsement for you..." Cliff interrupted.

"Because..." Ryan continued, "it would mean spending less time together. Admit it, Cliff...if you had to choose between a date with a new guy or watching *NCIS* with me...which would you pick?"

"That totally depends. Does the dude put out on the first date? And are we talking original series or Los Angeles? Because LL Cool J is fucking hot."

"Exactly, genius. The very fact you have to *think* about it proves my point. A normal dude would go for the date every time. We really are the old married couple everyone accuses us of being—you just don't want to admit it. You didn't even ask if it was a rerun."

Shaking his head at his friend's foolishness, Cliff grinned. "Okay, I give. You're going to talk me to death if we don't have sex. And you promise you're not going to divorce me if you hate it..." Cliff reached for the lube, but Ryan got there first.

"I do...and that question I asked earlier?"

"Oh my god, what question? You think I'm still capable of thought?" Cliff asked, nearly certain his balls were blue.

Ryan laughed. "That's good, because I've changed my mind about exploring. For now. Turn over, baby. I think I can figure this out."

Chapter Nine

Cliff's eyelids lowered and his cock twitched against Ryan's. For a moment Ryan was tempted to just squirt the lube over them both and give grinding a try. Then Cliff nodded once, so Ryan moved over, placing a hand on the taller man's hip as he shifted to his side then onto his belly.

"Talk to me, Cliff...tell me if I do something wrong." He squirted the lube onto his hand first and lightly brushed his fingers over Cliff's crack, over his balls, and forward between his legs to stroke the underside of his engorged length. Cliff's hips rose from the bed, granting him access, pumping into his fist, working up friction.

In this position, grabbing Cliff's cock from behind, it was the same grip he used on himself, and for a moment it was weird to be giving a hand job and not feel a thing.

Cliff looked back over his shoulder, and their gazes met. Ryan slid his hand back, spreading the lube, his fingers playing over the soft puckered skin that surrounded the tight ring of muscles. He felt rather than saw the twitch and quiver beneath his fingertips. When Cliff's ass chased his fingers, he slid in a single digit.

"Uhn…" Cliff said, hips pressing back. "Been a long time…"

Ryan moved in closer and ran his other hand over Cliff's lower back as he watched the glide in and out of Cliff's tight channel.

"You okay?" he asked after a minute.

"Two fingers now, Ry," Cliff panted, his hips moving. Pulling slowly out, Ryan added more lube, worried that he might be going too fast, then wanted to laugh at himself for his uncertainty. Cliff was a big boy; he'd tell him if he was doing something wrong.

Ryan pressed two very slick fingers to Cliff's pucker. As he eased them inside, a breath of air left Cliff and he pushed back into the movement. "Oh yeah…" he said on a low growl.

God, how Ryan loved that voice. It scraped and abraded, and reminded him this was all man beneath him. Not a substitute for something else, but the hard muscles, deep masculine voice, hairy-fucking-chest of the only man—only person—he wanted.

Pumping his fingers in and out, rubbing them together to create a little movement, twisting them left, then right. He catalogued every one of Cliff's reactions, noting what he seemed to like best, already planning how to make it better the next time. The man on his knees in front of him was spectacular. His muscles stood out in sharp relief, bulging and flexing as he supported himself and rocked with Ryan's movements. Cliff's weight shifted so he rested on one hand, and his broad shoulders rippled as the other hand started stroking his own cock.

"Now, Rhino...need you now," Cliff said with a hoarse snarl.

Slowly siding his fingers all the way out, Ryan moved between Cliff's legs. He added more lube, coating his eager erection in a better-safe-than-sore logic.

Cliff spread his knees wider then leaned down to rest his weight on his elbow. Ryan spread the solid cheeks wide with one hand and slid his cock over the tight hole, savoring every slick sensation.

With his target in sight, he lined himself up, touching his tip to Cliff's rim. For a moment he closed his eyes with the intensity of the feelings coursing through him, then his lids popped open. He didn't want to miss one second of this. The head of his cock met the resistance of Cliff's anus, and Ryan tentatively leaned forward, pressing until he breached the tight ring of muscle. With a soft grunt, the powerful man beneath him pushed back, driving himself farther onto Ryan's cock.

Ryan's eyes practically rolled back in his head from the intense spike of pleasure. Nothing in his life had ever felt so good as being sheathed in Cliff's silky heat. Shouting a curse, Ryan tried to rein in the all-consuming need to press forward, to bury himself before Cliff was ready. He tightened his grip on the base of his cock while Cliff's ass fluttered around him.

Digging his fingers into Cliff's hip, he drew his cock most of the way out then slid slowly back inside. Without a doubt this was the hottest, tightest hole he'd ever been inside, made all the better by the knowledge this was Cliff, his best friend, the one person who knew him, knew his secrets, and would always have his back.

"Unbelievable. Like falling through the rabbit hole," Ryan gritted as he drew back, then surged forward.

"Fucking unreal," Cliff agreed, apparently on the same page. Then Cliff's head turned and their mouths fused in a duel of tongues.

Although his brain wanted to draw the moment out, to stay here inside Cliff forever, his body had other needs, and his hips snapped forward. He pumped with an increasing sense of urgency, the strokes sure and strong, slamming farther into Cliff's ass on every downward slide. Rising back on his knees, he gripped Cliff's hips with both hands and started a pounding rhythm. His lover met him on each drive, grunts and groans surrounded them, their breath harsh, the sound of slapping skin punctuating each forceful plunge into the satin channel. Settling deeper and deeper, swallowed up by the heat, his body threatening to go supernova.

Cliff's hand moved faster, and Ryan covered it with his own as they flew together toward the finish line. The ache in his balls was intense as he soared closer to orgasm. Changing his motion, Ryan's hips moved in quick, shallow thrusts that caused Cliff to shout. With a grin, Ryan did it again, realizing he'd managed to find Cliff's gland.

"Cliff...baby...dayum...getting fucking tighter."

"Gonna come, Ry," Cliff grunted.

"Do it, honey. Let me feel you..."

When Cliff's channel started to clench and spasm around him, Ryan gave a few more quick snaps with his hips, then slid deep...all the way home. It didn't take anything more than knowing Cliff was coming while Ryan's cock pounded into him... His orgasm raced up his spine, his balls emptied in a jet. The cum exploded from the head of his cock, a pain-pleasure sensation that had his toes curling as he filled Cliff's ass.

*

With his ass still clenched in a post-orgasm lockdown, Cliff collapsed forward onto his stomach shifting just enough to avoid the wet spot and taking Ryan with him.

"Holy shit," Ryan said, his voice full of…wonder?

The sentiment so closely matched his own thoughts that Cliff began to laugh, which caused his muscles to contract and expel Ryan from his ass. Rather than moving away, Rhino slid to his side and remained close. A calloused hand rubbed over Cliff's lower back and cheeks.

"You okay?" Ryan asked softly. He trailed kisses over Cliff's shoulder. "I didn't hurt you, did I?"

Talking into his pillow, Cliff mumbled, "You know, in all the years we've known each other, I never would have pegged you as a post-coital snuggler."

"Mmm…" Ryan murmured. "And I didn't know you had a vocabulary that included post-coital."

"Was on a spelling test, I think."

"Hah. Hey, Cliff?"

"Yeah?"

"That was pretty fucking awesome."

Cliff closed his eyes and pressed his lips together to keep from saying something foolish. Like telling the man who'd fucked him into the mattress that he couldn't wait to do it again. That over the course of the last hour, everything in his life had been turned upside down by the knowledge that he loved Ryan.

Not loved as a fellow brother-in-arms. Not loved as a best friend. Love-loved as in the one person he wanted beside him for the rest of his life. He'd been arguing against that truth ever since Ryan had put him on his knees. Just to think that he could have Ryan in his mouth, in his ass, in his life forever…but that was something that wasn't ever going to happen. Their paths were no longer on an intersecting course, and he'd need to find a way to let Ryan go.

To make Rhino go…he still had a mission to complete.

Not wanting to raise the suspicions of the man who knew him better than anyone, Cliff kept his tone mild. "Yeah…I don't usually catch but it was pretty good," he agreed. He forced a yawn. "Rhino, don't take this the wrong way, but as glad as I am you enjoyed it, I'm wiped after the day I've had. Plus the drive home. Any chance that brain of yours is ready to shut down for the night so I can catch a few hours of sleep?"

In his imagination, the pause that followed his question was filled with hurt and unasked questions. Ryan's hand stilled, reversed direction, and traced along the bumps of Cliff's spine until he reached his neck. He drew his hand away for a minute. Cliff thought maybe Ryan would give him the last word and turn over to sleep. Or better yet, return to his own room, to give Cliff the space he badly needed right about now. He should have known better.

Rhino's hand fisted in Cliff's hair and he pulled hard enough to force his head around to meet his gaze. He knew if it had been light enough in the room he'd see the gold flecks blazing in the hazel eyes.

"Tell yourself any lie you want to, Cliff, if you think it will make you feel better. Just remember, I know you as well as you know me…maybe better. You might run, but you'll never be able to hide. I'll just drag your ass back. To me."

His lips closed over Cliff's, mashing them so hard their teeth bumped. Then his mouth softened, their lips parting, Ryan's tongue seeking his. Cliff fisted his hands beneath his pillow to keep from reaching for Ryan—this gentle kiss so much more devastating to the steel he tried to wrap around his heart.

Chapter Ten

Cliff's eyes flashed open, his senses instantly alert for any sign of trouble, momentarily confused by the heavy weight across his legs and the pain in his ass. Until he remembered that pain had a name: Ryan Matthews. It had been a long time since he'd awakened with someone in his bed. As Ryan had reminded him last night—thank you very much—it had been years since he'd even had a second date. Now he was in bed with his straight best friend, and seriously hoping things weren't going to be FUBAR between them.

Climbing from the bed, Cliff grabbed his gear and padded silently from the room and the nearly overwhelming temptation to offer his ass up for a second time. Briefly considering going to breakfast at the main house and possibly delay talking to Rhino for a few more hours, Cliff discarded the idea as pointless. The stubborn ass would only follow, and god knew Ryan was perfectly capable of bringing up the intimate details of the previous night in front of every person seated at the table. And what had he said last night about Ty? If that fucking squid was behind this…

Ignoring the call of the coffee pot, Cliff leaned over and laced his boots. A ten-mile run would clear his head and hopefully Ryan would wake up and remember an urgent errand in Coronado. That would be the best outcome for their current situation.

Ryan was right about one thing…Cliff knew him well. He recognized the restlessness in his friend and knew this was a vulnerable time. He'd just returned from a six-month deployment and was facing the first real decision of his career about whether or not to re-enlist.

Until you hit twenty years, there wasn't a helluva lot to consider. Now with Cliff heading to Civland, Ryan would be facing the rest of his Navy career without his best friend. No wonder he felt some hesitation about his reenlistment. It was only natural.

With his own uncertain future, Cliff's inclination was to share his thoughts with Ryan. They'd always bounced ideas off one another, but Ryan could never resist trying to solve a problem of this magnitude. He'd become so invested in fixing things for Cliff, he'd lose sight of what was best for himself and his career. It would be an absolutely unfair way to repay two decades of friendship.

"Running away?" Ryan said from the doorway. Cliff had been so preoccupied with his thoughts he hadn't even heard Rhino get out of bed.

"Nope, just running. Wanna tag along?" he asked, just as he always did, knowing full well Ryan hated to run, especially early in the morning.

Rhino's eyes narrowed and he stared at Cliff for a long ten count, then nodded. "Give me five. How far?"

"Ten miles. More or less."

"I vote less. Boots, huh? Never mind—makes sense in this landscape. Be right there." He was back in four, stepping onto the porch while still clipping his iPod to the band strapped to his arm.

"About last night—" Cliff started, hoping he could get Ryan to say whatever it was he had in mind before they started running.

"It was great," Ryan said casually, then leaned down to tie the laces on his boots, his tight ass showcased in a pair of skimpy running shorts.

Dirty pool.

Cliff opened his mouth, but his phone chirped before he had a chance to say anything. Ryan straightened and for a moment their eyes met, a dozen different memories of emergency mission call-outs flashing between them.

Snatching his new iPhone from the holster, he glanced at the caller ID. "San Diego PD," he told Ryan.

"Snyder," he said by way of greeting. He turned his back on Ryan as he listened to Detective Wagner talk, asking one or two questions, but the outcome was inevitable. When he ended the call, he faced Ryan once again. "First, I know you want to talk, Rhino, and right now, that's just not going to happen. The SDPD wants me back there to do a walk-through of the club before they turn the keys over to me…"

"To you? Why would they give you the keys?"

"That's the part I should have told you last night but something…came up." He smiled despite his unease with their situation. "Detective Wagner, the one in charge of the investigation, had me look through a dozen mug books before sending me on a covert mission"—he rolled his eyes—"that ended at New Horizons rehab hospital, behind a guarded door. Draco Kincaid survived the shooting, although he'll probably never walk again."

"Aww…fuck me."

"Yeah. Wagner questioned us together, watching us like we knew more than we were letting on. Obviously Draco does, but I'm still in the dark. But he did ask me to close up his business, post signs, make sure everything got cleaned up." Cliff shrugged a shoulder. "That was it until the end. I managed a quick hug and Draco whispered he wanted to see you when you got back CONUS. I should have told you last night but…"

Rhino blinked, his face a careful mask. "You were a bit distracted. All right, I have the basics, but that was pretty damned early for a casual phone call. When does Wagner expect you?"

"Today…at sixteen hundred." Cliff looked at his watch. "Plenty of time…"

"Is Draco under guard?"

"Yeah, a fresh-faced undercover from the gang unit. I think Wagner is mostly relying on word of Draco's death to keep him safe. No sense in looking for a dead man."

"No, but there is a reason to look for a previously unknown witness. The asshole is setting you up…"

"I realize that. Which is why I want on the road in the next thirty minutes. He won't expect me there before noon. I'll get inside, have a good look around. That still leaves me time to find a vantage point where I can track who arrives before I decide to show myself."

"All right, let's go. We need to stop by my place for some weapons—you don't have shit here."

"You searched— Never mind, that's not important—and it just means you didn't find my stash. Listen up, Rhino, because we are on a nonnegotiable point here. This is where we part ways, my friend. There are a million things I wish I could say—but I can't. Not now—there isn't time, and hell…it's probably better this way.

"Go back to the base…talk to the skipper and take those orders, man. You need to do it for you. Shit…you need to do it for me. Six is something we always talked about, and if you don't take this opportunity, you'll always wonder—what if…"

Ryan's face remained a mask, but Cliff pressed forward. He wasn't offering a choice, he was telling him the way it was going to be.

"I'll take care of whatever Draco needs. My guess is he knows who did this and wants justice. I can give him that—you give me Six. When you come back…"

They stared at each other a long moment without speaking. Ryan's face was like chiseled granite, his hazel eyes muddy, his jaw working like maybe he'd already popped in a stick of the ever-present gum. Or else there were words trying to fight their way out. Either way, the early morning bristle over the hard jaw drew Cliff's gaze and his throat tightened at the loss for what they might have been…

"Don't, Ry. Whatever you're planning…please, for me, just let it go. You'll never know how much the last two days have meant to me. This"—he gestured with his thumb and pinkie—"this friendship is the best thing in my life. I need us to keep it—but I need you to stay out of this mess.

"I fucked up, and my lack of judgment cost me—but if the mistake had been in the field, the price could have been a life. The price isn't too high. I keep my record, my retirement. I was on my last tour anyway. But I still want one thing, Ry. I want you to try for Six. I need to know you're still living our dreams."

For a slow count to ten and back again, neither of them moved, then with a sharp nod of agreement, Ryan stepped forward and gave him a slap on the shoulder.

"What can I do to help you get out of here? Are you taking everything or just going for the night?"

"I think it's best if I take it all. Draco offered an apartment on the top floor of his place and I'm gonna crash there until I figure this out. "

"And the mystery weapons cache? Although I suspect you were bullshitting me."

"Nope. There are actually two. One in the Jeep. The other I sorta cheated on, since you wouldn't have had enough time to check everything. There's a built-in safe."

"Show me…"

"I will, but first—" He glanced over to the main house where a steady stream of men were going in through the kitchen entrance for breakfast. "Let me say good-bye to Ty and Cass. If you could grab my shit? I only have the two bags…"

Thirty minutes later, he was on his way. Cliff's relief at Ryan's acceptance of his decision was tempered by the sensation that he'd just ripped out his heart and left it back at the WSR.

"Be safe, Rhino…" Those were shitty last words to say to the man who owned his heart, but they'd been all he had.

Chapter Eleven

Despite giving Ryan the impression that Detective Wagner might be slightly less than competent, Cliff was fairly certain the man would be expecting him to show up early and case the building. He wouldn't have called to set up the meeting at four until he had eyes on the club. It was what Cliff would have done—and he didn't think Kam missed much. So assuming he was walking into a trap was easy, identifying just how big a trap was harder.

There was no reason to think Cliff had anything to do with the robbery-murder, so it was probably just as he—and Rhino—figured. Word would have already been leaked that there was a witness who could identify the killers and that Wagner was meeting him at the club later this afternoon. There'd only been one guard on Draco, no second detective over a week into the investigation. The nature of the club would make it a too-hot-to-handle political hot potato, so Cliff would operate on the theory that other than the guard at the rehab, Wagner was damn likely to be working alone. There was also that weird little scene at the PD with Detective Kingston. Something not right there. A leak inside the PD? Maybe.

Whenever they were given a mission, a SEAL team trained long and hard, perfecting their plan based on all available data on the target and location. They trained harder for how to survive once everything about the plan got fucked up. Because the only easy day was yesterday—had to be, otherwise you wouldn't be here to tackle today's shit, right?

So yeah, Cliff would have preferred more than a few hours lead time, could have used a set of floor plans for the structure, and would have loved some backup. But that wasn't the way today was going to go, so there was nothing to be gained by dwelling on it. He wasn't going to get to move under the cover of night, there weren't secret underground tunnels to infiltrate, just a decades-old brick building set in the middle of the busy San Diego historic warehouse district—practically in the shadows of Petco Park baseball stadium. It made camouflage a moot point. After a quick stop at his apartment, he'd donned the uniform of the day—boots, jeans, T-shirt, a body armor vest to carry his equipment, and the loose-fitting windbreaker to hide it all. The Padres ball cap was a bonus.

From a parking structure down the block, Cliff spotted security cameras located on the north and east side of the structure. Draco was a former SEAL and not stupid, so with little wiggle room in his schedule, Cliff made the logical assumption the camera coverage would be consistent around the perimeter. From this distance, the windows looked very much like the windows of the surrounding converted warehouses: large, showroom-sized that would let in plenty of light.

In reality, due to the nature of the business, the first floor windows were actually boarded over and painted on the interior of the building, then draped with fabric to give the impression of curtained windows where none existed. The space between the reinforced glass and the interior wood gave Hard Labour the opportunity to blend in with their more…refined neighbors. From the sidewalk level, pedestrians were treated to museum-quality artifacts from the early days of San Diego, the California Gold Rush, and the Mexican-American War. Even though Draco purchased the club a decade before the ballpark had led the way to revitalizing the old warehouse district, it paid to blend in. After all, he'd need to remain on the right side of city hall if he wanted to renew his business and liquor licenses.

He trained his field glasses on the second floor, identifying the office where the shootings had occurred, plus what appeared to be several other empty rooms. He remembered his brief glimpse down the short hallway from the other night. At a guess he'd say most of the space was either vacant or storage. The third floor was unexplored territory that had undergone some initial transformation since the last time Cliff had been to the club with Ryan more than a year previously. The windows were new, as were several balconies. The exterior brick had been cleaned and there was spots of darker clay where repair work had been completed. He studied each of the windows carefully, looking for any sign of occupation. Draco's invitation to stay in an apartment within the building introduced concerns of tenants as innocent bystanders if today went TU.

From his vantage point, the apartments appeared vacant, with only the corner unit above the office showing signs of furniture. Probably where Draco lived. Maybe this conversion to individual units was why Draco was getting out of the club scene.

After identifying all the areas of egress on this side of the building, Cliff selected his entrance, removed a small length of detonation cord from one of the many pockets on his vest, then zipped his jacket. Now that he'd made his choice, the plan was to get inside as quickly as possible. If Kam Wagner was already inside, he'd remain hidden, giving Cliff plenty of rope to hang himself, because the detective would be interested to see how Cliff was involved with Draco. Too bad for Kam, because all he'd catch Cliff at this afternoon was walking through the building to get a feel for the place. Until he had a chance to talk with Draco privately, he was unlikely to discover anything significant. Certainly not the motive behind the shooting.

One thing Cliff would stake his life on—those men were there for the disk, not a previously undisclosed amount of cash. They'd been not much more than hired thugs, and if they'd found a hundred grand in the safe, one of them would have said something.

With a casual gait that was deceptively quick, he made his way down the emergency stairs of the garage, then wound his way through a narrow alley between two commercial structures. He passed through one unlocked gate, a sharp kick opened another, until he was at a partially concealed steel door on the back side of Hard Labour. There were two empty parking slots, which most likely made it the private entrance for the owner. With no time to worry if someone was watching, he wrapped the det cord around the lock, stepped back, then said a silent prayer for no audible alarms.

With a sound not much louder than a pat of butter hitting a skillet, the charge did its job. Cliff opened the door and stepped inside, pulling it closed behind him. He blinked into the dim interior, and wished he could have brought his night-vision goggles. Two steps later air brushed against his neck, and Cliff ducked and whirled.

A familiar bark of laughter rolled across his skin. "About fucking time you got here."

*

"God, I love to make an entrance," Rhino said, his laughter spilling out. Cliff's jaw flopped open and his eyes grew wide as his gaze met Ryan's.

"You are a certifiable ass. Didn't you hear a thing I said back at the WSR?"

"Eh? What's that? Can't hear you…" Ryan cupped his ear, leaning forward like an old man. He knew he was being an ass, but Cliff had pissed him the fuck off when he'd told him to butt out, like he had an exclusive right to make decisions regarding the two of them.

Before Ryan could continue his antics, Cliff grabbed him by the shoulders and shook him hard. Leaning in, he put his mouth close enough that his breath tickled Ryan's ear. "Shut the fuck up."

Ryan jerked back but Cliff's fingers tightened, and a flush crawled up his neck. It was as angry as Ryan had ever seen his friend…and after twenty years, that was saying something.

"What the fuck is wrong with you? We have no idea who's in here—I've never known you to be so goddam careless on a mission," Cliff whispered.

"No, actually you haven't ever known me to be careless, which if you were thinking with your brain instead of your emotions would tell you something. Drop your mission mentality for half a minute and think. Would I be standing here talking to you if I thought either of us could possibly be in danger? Draco has state of the art security installed and I checked the monitors. I'm pretty sure no one's been here since yesterday when a man I assume is your Detective Wagner reset the alarms. How come you didn't mention he was hot?"

Although Ryan had done a cursory run-through of the building, he still kept his voice low—there hadn't been time to check every closet or other potential hiding place.

Cliff's brows lowered and nearly met in the middle as he frowned at Ryan. Then his hands dropped to his sides, his fingers curling into fists, and Ryan debated stepping out of arm's reach until he cooled down. "How did you get here before me?"

Ryan shrugged. "I paced you all the way back. As soon as I confirmed you took the turnoff to your apartment, I came here and let myself in with a key..."

"You have a key and decided not to mention it because…"

"Because you were being a stubborn ass and making decisions on my behalf. This isn't the time or place, but we *are* going to talk. You don't get to decide what I do next, Cliff. I might love you—even though I don't have a goddamn clue what that means—but you're not the one who gives orders here. Now did you have something in particular you wanted to look at while we're here—before the cute detective arrives?"

Cliff's jaw snapped shut and Ryan had a hard time not laughing at the stubborn press of lips.

"All right, you're pissed…so noted for the record. I've walked through the first floor and haven't seen anything unusual on the premises. I've also checked the security feed from the cameras. There're only three saved files since the shooting by the way, the police took everything else. Your detective is the one who's showing up at seventeen hundred each day to change out the tape. Seems he believes the killers might return and he wants to know what they look like. Good plan as far as it goes. Follow me."

Without waiting for a response, Ryan turned and led the way to a door carved underneath the staircase and tapped in a code on the keypad. At the quiet tick of the lock mechanism, he pushed his way inside and waited for Cliff to follow.

Cliff's head swiveled left and right as he took in the impressive array of video monitors displaying the exterior of the building. "Good setup. Okay, so this is the control center that feeds the security monitors I saw in Draco's office. Are there any shots from the interior? Did they capture the shooters on screen?"

"The interior cameras are only in the play areas of the club and camouflaged to maintain the illusion of privacy. Draco would've had a revolt by most of his customers if they thought he taped their games, but he'd said it was necessary to protect his assets. There aren't any cameras in place in the staff areas. The exterior is locked up by the angles—no way in or out without getting seen. Makes you wonder why the PD had you looking through the photos, doesn't it? They damn sure should've had a perfect shot of the shooters coming and going."

Moving to the control board, Ryan pulled up the view from the camera at the owner's entrance. With a few keystrokes, he rolled back the time setting to the few minutes before he arrived on scene, then digitally spliced an empty shot to remove any evidence of either of them arriving.

"Nice...I wonder if we can get a copy of the confiscated video from the night of the shooting?"

"I'm pretty sure there's a digital recovery on this system. I might be able to retrieve the files once the cop leaves. I'll try if you want?"

"Yeah—thanks…" Cliff moved toward the door, then stopped with his hand resting on the frame. "Ryan…"

Ducking underneath Cliff's arm, Ryan trotted up the stairs then waited on the landing. When Cliff trudged up behind him, Ryan bit back his smile. Still keeping his voice low, he gestured down the hall. "This staircase only leads to Draco's office and a few storerooms. Access to the rest of the second and third floor is from staircases external to the club area to maintain privacy. Except for the owner's elevator, which you can access behind the bookcase inside the office."

"You checked the storerooms?" Cliff asked, maintaining his all-business expression.

"Not yet. I haven't been upstairs either. How do you want to handle it?"

Cliff stared down the hall, his eyes narrowed as he assessed the situation. "Four rooms. You take left, I'll take right—let's clear them, then the office." He drew his SIG and screwed on the suppressor. Ryan did likewise.

"How certain are you the detective isn't already in here? I'd hate to shoot him accidentally."

Ryan shrugged. "He could have done the same splicing I did to hide his arrival, but since it would raise questions about tampering with evidence, my gut says we're alone. Besides, the place felt…empty.

Can't be positive unless we clear every room. My guess is he's watching from outside."

On a silent nod, both men serious now that weapons were drawn, they moved in tandem down the short hallway. It took less than five minutes to verify three of the rooms were empty, and the fourth contained stacks of white cardboard bankers boxes, each labelled with a year—presumably the date of the records within.

"Why would they leave these boxes? Isn't this evidence of some sort?" Ryan whispered.

"The crime scene is Draco's office, so even though they would have checked every room in the building, it's not likely they could take anything not directly related to the shooting. I suppose they'll dig further into the club background if the investigation wears on?"

"I guess," Ryan said. "Man, we've got a lot to learn if we're going to be PIs once we retire…"

"Shut the fuck up, Rhino. You've got a job to finish," Cliff said, although a smile played about his lips at the reference to one of many post-Navy careers they'd discussed over the years. Private investigator usually came up after a few too many brews while binge-watching *NCIS*.

Cliff checked his watch. "Let's look at the office, then…you said there's an elevator in there?"

"Yeah. Maybe we can hit the third floor quick and be back downstairs before your detective arrives. Since Draco gave you free run of the place we'll have plenty of time to look around after he officially turns the keys over. Speaking of which…why'd you blow the door?"

"I was in a hurry. Besides, I didn't blow it—much. Just took out the locking mechanism. It's repairable. Come on, let's hurry."

Moving quickly, they closed the door behind themselves, then using hand signals, they counted down before bursting into the office, weapons at the ready.

Blood still stained the floor, although someone had cleaned up the biohazards. Draco would no doubt be getting a bill from the local crime scene decontamination contractors. From the angle of the stain, Ryan could visualize where the bartender had fallen, just inside the door. Circumventing the dark mark on the cheap carpet, he stepped farther into the room, aware of Cliff's presence behind him.

As before, Ryan went left and Cliff right until they cleared the space. When he got to the partially open bookcase, Ryan ducked behind it and stood looking at the bed for a long moment. An ugly heat burned low in his belly when he thought of Cliff lying here, cuffed to Draco's headboard. Pressing his lips tight together to keep from saying anything stupid like—

from now on my bed is the only one you'll be cuffed to— he flipped on the light switch then crossed to where the elevator doors were partially concealed behind a trifold screen. He pushed the button and they slid open noiselessly.

"I didn't even know that was there," Cliff said quietly from the entry.

Ryan turned and walked back to the main part of the office, needing to be away from the bed and the unwelcome images of a bound and submissive Cliff.

"Ryan? Tell me again why you're here?"

Meeting his friend's light steel-gray eyes, Ryan waited a beat before he answered. Cliff's once dark hair was definitely more salt and pepper now, and longer than he usually wore it. He'd been up and getting ready for a run early this morning, with no time for a shave, so his jaw was scruffy and begged for Ryan to touch it, to feel the bristle beneath his palms. The loose-fitting windbreaker did little to disguise the solid build of the man, even under his body armor. Everything about Cliff was just…right.

Why hadn't he realized this sooner? His heart seemed ready to gallop away, the beat of his pulse sounding loud in his ears. Moistening his lips, Ryan stalled for time, forgetting for a moment what the question was.

"You're still active duty, Ry…and with your new orders…this really is a situation you shouldn't be involved in. I appreciate you going through the building with me, but seriously, you need to go before Wagner gets here and officially makes you part of the case. This is something I can handle alone."

Ryan blinked once, then the truest words he'd ever spoken seemed to tumble out of his mouth. "You're never going to be alone as long as I'm alive."

*

Cliff stared at Ryan, trying to make sense of the words coming out of his friend's mouth. It was the second time he'd said something to shock Cliff since he'd arrived...twenty minutes ago? Before he could ask for clarification, the quiet vibration of his phone against his hip drew his attention. Since he'd had to replace his SEAL issue special communications equipment during his retirement processing, the list of people who had the number could be counted on one hand—Detective Kam Wagner being the first one who came to mind. Cursing the interruption, he snatched the phone and checked the caller ID. Shit. He had to take the call.

He glared at Ryan. "We're not finished with this. You hold that fucking thought," he growled out. "Snyder," he snapped into the phone.

"You've got two coming in through the front with automatic weapons. Jesus-fucking-Christ. Go into the private elevator in Draco's office and lock it down between floors. Shit, Snyder. I'm coming in behind them but reinforcements are three minutes out—"

"Wait outside for backup, Wagner. You're outgunned and I'm safe...you hear me? Fucking wait outside." Cliff punched the end button and dropped the phone in his windbreaker pocket, already heading for the door. "We've got two targets, carrying automatic weapons of unknown type. Coming in through the front door. Not sure how much time we've got. I'm going to hold them until backup arrives. As soon as I have them pinned, you get clear. No vest, no target practice. Non-fucking-negotiable, Rhino—disappear."

Any response was lost in the sound of the front door glass shattering under a sudden burst of automatic fire that announced the arrival of the would-be attackers. Apparently no time at all was how much they had.

Cliff dove through the doorway, counting on the fact the sound of his movement would be masked because the assholes would have ruined their hearing when they fired. Rolling away from the office door, he came to a stop at the top of the landing and risked a quick look over the stairs. Two men dressed in stocking caps, cammie pants, and black T-shirts held

AK47s waist high as they scanned the room. Ducking out of sight of the men below, Cliff used hand signals to indicate there were two men, two weapons. He didn't bother to turn to see if Ryan was behind him—the signals were standard ops, and Ryan would stick around until he knew Cliff had the situation controlled.

With help on the way, it would be preferable to avoid using his weapon. He was concealed carry permitted in California, but he'd prefer to avoid drawing further scrutiny from the SDPD. He also needed to keep the assholes downstairs to make things easier for the locals. The thoughts flashed through his mind even as his body was putting his plan into action.

Switching the SIG to his left hand, he reached into his vest and removed a flashbang with his right. He risked another look and saw both men's heads turn toward the opening where a glass door and privacy vestibule had once stood.

Kam Wagner ran toward the doorway, his badge in one hand, his service revolver in the other. His mouth moved, clearly shouting but the words were indistinguishable. The fool hadn't heeded Cliff's advice to wait outside. He intended to stage a one-man rescue.

As if in slow motion, the two men raised their weapons and started to turn. Kam was unprotected—

a clear shot through the open doorway. Cliff pulled the pin on the stun grenade with his teeth, then memorizing the position of the two men relative to the rest of the room, he closed his eyes and tossed the device ten feet behind them. The blast was deafening, but before the flash even burned out, Cliff was up and firing his weapon, registering the second set of gunshots coming from his left.

"Target acquired," Ryan said quietly when they stopped firing.

Cliff never hesitated. He turned to Ryan. "Give me your gun," he ordered, snatching it from Ryan's hand. He pointed it to the mess downstairs and fired it once, making sure there wouldn't be any doubts he'd fired both weapons. "Get out of here now, Ry. There's nothing to show you were here. Go to McP's," he said, referring to the SEAL hang out in Coronado. There would be plenty of willing witnesses to Rhino's presence.

Ryan stared at him, his large hazel eyes looking nearly brown in the gloom of the hallway. His lips parted, but Cliff couldn't let him speak. Not right now.

Sirens could be heard, echoing off the buildings, there would only be seconds left.

"Ry, if you care about me even a little, then do this for me. Please? I'll be okay, everything here is justifiable—and it's going to take days to clear up.

You can't afford to be involved right now. Get out before anyone sees you. There's a way off the roof and you know it…" He reached for Ryan's face, but dropped his hand before touching him. "Please," he repeated softly.

Nodding once, Ryan pressed a quick kiss to Cliff's mouth. "Meet me at SEAL Beach next Tuesday. Zero-five-hundred. I'll be waiting." Then he turned and ran through the door to the office.

Underneath the wail of sirens, tires screeched on the pavement, and dozens of car doors open, voices shouted. Cliff stayed put, not wanting to draw friendly fire from a wannabe hero. Finally someone seemed to be in charge, as he heard the distinctive click of an amplified bullhorn.

"Police—you're surrounded. Throw down your weapons and come out with your hands up."

Chapter Twelve

Cliff stared at the papers spread on the dining room table and tried to work up some enthusiasm for creating a pros and cons list on his yellow legal pad. Stifling a yawn, he ignored the pen and reached for his coffee instead. Considering how late he'd arrived the night before, he deserved to have at least two cups of coffee before he started the intimidating task of deciding what to do with the rest of his life.

A quick tap on the door was all the warning he got before it swung open.

"Mind if we come in?" Ty asked, stepping through the doorway without actually waiting for an answer. Cass followed close on his heels, a bronze-toned travel mug in his hands.

"Hey, Cliff, welcome back," Cass said. "I wasn't sure we'd be seeing you again so soon. Glad you could get away."

The two men joined him at the small table. Cass leaned forward and picked up a map of downtown San Diego. Ty glanced at it, then turned his bright blue gaze on Cliff.

"You look like shit, jarhead."

"You look fat and happy, squid."

They grinned at each other, but Cass shook his head. "I didn't think Marines could be in the SEALs."

"They can't," Ty and Cliff said together.

Ty leaned back and took up the tale. "Cliff joined the Corps first, then had to get out when he discovered exactly that."

"Ty never lets me forget it."

"Hell, man, you never forget it. I see you went back to the high and tight," Ty teased, referring to his recent haircut.

"Not exactly." He rubbed a hand over his brush cut and was hit with a sudden memory of Ryan's fingers twisted into his hair... "I didn't go as short as usual. And to be honest, I don't actually know what else to ask for at the barber shop," he admitted.

Cass pressed open the map and peered at the scale illustration of downtown San Diego. His finger traced the path from Petco Park to the building that housed Hard Labour, then over the water to the base.

"San Diego's a great city. Have you decided what you're going to do?"

"Hah..." Cliff pushed back his chair before standing and walking to the kitchen to pour a cup of coffee. He held the carafe in the air. "Anyone else?"

Receiving two head shakes, he returned the pot to the maker then leaned his hips on the counter and blew out a breath. "That's the question of the day...isn't it? I don't suppose Whit's job is still available?" he said, half-joking. "Not that I know anything about horses, not like he did—but I can learn. And god knows I can shovel shit..."

Ty's palm landed on the table with a slap, but Cass merely covered his lover's hand and gave a squeeze.

"Huh...well, I admit, you are pretty good at that. But, most of my hands have a bit more experience in ranch life beyond mucking stalls.

"Don't take this the wrong way, Cliff, because if you need a job or a place to stay—then this is it. We told you when you called yesterday that you're always welcome here, and we meant it. I just always pictured you as more of a beach person. Lord knows we have all the sand you could ever want for running, but don't you swim just about every day? We don't even have a pool for laps."

"Triathlons," Ty fake-coughed.

As a lifelong resident of San Diego—except for the short periods when he'd been stationed elsewhere, there were certain things he'd miss about the Southern California community if he left. But there were complications now, particularly given what happened at Hard Labour and his forced retirement.

"I thought about settling in San Diego, sure. To be honest, I have no real ties there. My family's in Santa Barbara, and we're not close. I sold my house before my last deployment, because I'd planned to buy a condo when I returned. Now I'm in an apartment complex and with all the twenty-somethings running around half-dressed—not that I mind looking—but damn, it makes me feel older by the day.

"I'm not rich, but I'm not strapped for cash either. Obviously I don't have a job—not even any real industry that I'm tied to. Basically, this is a time in my life for me to make big changes without disrupting anything."

His mind shied away from last Tuesday morning, when he'd had a chance at making a big change. Telling himself he was only going for a run, he'd driven past SEAL Beach and seen Rhino's Jeep in the lot. Not trusting he'd be able to say no again to Ryan, Cliff had kept driving until he'd stopped for breakfast near Carpenteria. Surprising everyone—including himself—he'd actually stopped in to see his parents. It had been a good reunion, but had also confirmed they had little in common once the first thirty minutes of conversation was finished.

He'd been ignoring the missed call notifications on his phone ever since.

Ty wrestled his hand free from Cass and flipped through the disorganized stack on the table.

"Newspapers, catalogs, maps, real estate magazines…and your trusty legal pad. You really that clueless?"

"Kiss my ass, Cookie—I'm looking at options."

"What about Rhino? What's he say?"

Unwilling to give Ty the opening he was digging for, Cliff shook his head. "Rhino's taking his orders to Six—I saw him on the schedule for a re-enlistment physical when I was finishing my retirement drill. My shit's all done with the Navy—this is his time to shine."

What about Rhino? The question had rattled around inside his head for the past week—and as much as he wished there was such a thing as happily ever after, that kind of shit didn't happen. Half the gay men he knew had gay-for-you fantasies. There was just something sexy about a straight guy coming to play on your equipment, but he'd been frustratingly unable to relegate what happened between him and Ry to a simple X-rated one-off between friends. He never should have agreed to the BJ, because from that moment on, nothing in Cliff's brain had worked right. He'd been unable to think of a single sexual encounter that had been better. Hell—that had even been close.

How could he have done something so impossible as falling in love with his straight best friend? The sex between them had been off the charts, but that wasn't even what had done it for Cliff. It had been that moment of absolute certainty that his world was perfectly in order when he'd awakened with Ryan in his bed. He wasn't stupid enough to fall for the if-you-love-him-let-him-go romantic tripe—that wasn't what this was about.

Cliff had fucked up at the end of his career—cut it short by a couple of years, but he had no regrets about what he'd accomplished in twenty-two total years of service. A minor aw-shit at the end couldn't take any of that away.

But Rhino? He was something special in the field and this was an opportunity he'd earned.

A downside of having a best friend was sometimes they knew what you wanted better than you did yourself. Cliff knew. Ryan had always wanted these orders to Six—*always*. They might be coming late in his career, but Ryan deserved this opportunity and Cliff would do everything he could—including ripping out his own heart—to make sure Ryan got a chance at his dream.

"Look, I appreciate everything you two have done for me. And you're right. I'm probably not cut out to be a cowboy, Cass. I'm not as hopeless as you're trying to make me out to be," he said with a smile aimed at Ty.

Gesturing at the pile on the table, he said, "There really are a lot of possibilities, including a job offer. I just want to take a few days to sort things out."

Sounds in the desert carried. Cliff had barely been aware of the comforting background noise he'd come to associate with ranch life at the WSR: the occasional sound of men shouting to each other, a lazy drone of a tractor in the distance, the whinny of a horse. Now another sound entered his consciousness. A sound as familiar as that of his own vehicle. Rhino's Jeep. His gaze locked with Ty's.

"You sonofabitch. You called him."

Ty's mouth curved up on one side in a lazy half-smile. "Ya think?"

Cliff straightened and set his coffee on the counter with a thunk.

"Hold on there, Cliff," Cass said. "Goddamn it, Ty, quit yanking his chain. Tyler didn't call anybody. Ryan called late last night to confirm you arrived safely. We assumed you told him you were coming until—"

"Until this morning when stupid shit started pouring out of your mouth," Ty finished.

"That's our cue to leave. Come on, Ty…" Cass stood, keeping a tight grip on his lover's hand.

Moving slowly, Ty rose, glanced down at the littered surface of the table once again, his lip curled into a snarl.

"There are two things in life I truly hate," he said as the sound of the Jeep pulling up outside carried in through the windows. "One, is when someone tries to decide what's best for me and pushes his solution at me, expecting I'll fall in line with the plan." His gaze flicked to Cass for a moment, and Cliff caught the ghost of a smile that flitted across the tall cowboy's face. There was obviously a story there...

"The other thing I can't stand is a coward. You think you can manage to tell Ryan how you feel and live with the consequences? The only easy day was yesterday, Cliff. Hooyah?"

Without waiting for a response, Ty turned and tugged Cass's hand. Cliff followed the two men as they exited through the front door.

"Hey, Rhino. Good to see you," Cass said as he and Ty stopped long enough to shake Ryan's hand after he climbed from the Jeep.

"Good to be here," he replied. Then with the deliberate movements of a sharpshooter, Ryan shifted his aim to look directly at Cliff. For a long moment, nothing penetrated Cliff's consciousness except the heat and determination contained in that gaze. It was as if Ryan could see straight through to his soul. And he probably could. Ryan knew him better than anyone. Knew exactly what Cliff had been trying to do. Knew exactly how Cliff felt about him. Maybe even already knew what Cliff was going to do with his future.

A shiver raced up his spine at the lazy curve of Ryan's lips.

"Hooyah," Cliff murmured.

*

For all their talk that they knew each other, Ryan hadn't been sure until this minute how Cliff would react to his showing up, unannounced. As if he'd given him a choice.

This morning Cliff looked good enough to eat— something he planned on doing shortly—with his hair back in a familiar brush cut, his pale steel eyes, the dark shadow of a beard covering his hard jaw.

Cliff stepped inside, and Ry followed right on his heels. He paused at the table, eyeing the stacks of maps and papers.

"We're going to talk about this later."

"Don't you think we should talk first?"

"Why? We both know I'm not going anywhere. Except after you. Get in the bedroom and get undressed."

"I'm not your sub, Ryan." Nevertheless he followed Ry's directions until he stood in front of the bed, shirt off, his running shorts pooled around his ankles before he seemed to realize what he was doing. Then he froze, except for a telltale flicker of his tongue to moisten his lips.

"Maybe not," Ryan said with a careless shrug. "Maybe you will be someday. Or just sometimes. Who cares? If we decide that's a route we want to explore, we will."

"So you're saying you'd be here even if I don't let you dominate me?"

Ryan pushed hard and Cliff fell backward onto the mattress. Without waiting to be invited, Ryan quickly stripped then scrambled up to straddled Cliff's hips.

"I'm saying I plan to do whatever I need to until we get it through your thick head that whatever the next step we take, it's going to be together."

"When do you leave?"

Ryan popped him on the forehead with the palm of his hand. "Pay attention, Cliff. I'm. Not. Leaving."

"But your orders..."

"Are to the Fleet Reserve."

"But you were on the physical list..."

"For a retirement physical, asshole. Dammit, Cliff...what's it going to take? Have I ever once made you a promise I didn't keep? Have I shown myself to be untrustworthy? What can I say to make you understand this is it for me... I told you, I'm not leaving you."

Cliff sucked in his breath in a sharp gasp. The moment stretched as Ryan stared into Cliff's eyes. Then he realized exactly what Cliff needed to hear— and he was ready to say it. He reached for Cliff's hands and threaded their fingers together, then slowly raised Cliff's arms until the backs of his hands pressed against the mattress. He leaned into the grip and squeezed tight.

"I love you, Cliff. As my friend. As my lover. As my forever."

Cliff's lips parted slightly, as if on a question, but Ryan captured them with his mouth instead, wanting to taste the answer on a kiss. Cliff's mouth opened, their tongues tangled in a sweet heat, and Ryan fell into the kiss.

The moan that spilled from Cliff's throat made Ryan want to sink into him right then, without another word, to join together until everything else except the two of them ceased to exist.

For just a moment, Cliff's muscles went lax beneath him, then executing a perfect kip up, he went from supine to upright, flipping Ryan on his back, effectively reversing their positions.

"It's easy to say that when you're on top, *baby.*" Cliff's voice already growly, seemed to come from somewhere near his toes and the emphasis on Ryan's favorite endearment wasn't quite happy.

"Cliff?"

"You don't get it, Ryan. It doesn't matter if you suddenly just decided you're bisexual—the minute we're together, people are going to think you're gay. Are you really ready for that? And yeah, it might have been hot as hell when you fucked me, but, Rhino…" Cliff took a deep breath, making a visible effort to calm himself.

"Honey," Cliff said, as if trying it out, and the word gave Ryan hope. "It's not the same kind of relationship you're used to. Yeah, I'm going to sound sexist here, or gay-centric, or some damned term...but the relationships aren't the same."

"Don't you think I know that?" Ryan asked.

"No, I don't think you do. Look, when you walk into a restaurant with a woman, people make certain assumptions—"

"Cliff—we've been walking into restaurants together for years. Don't you think people have made assumptions?"

"Sure, but they've never been true before, so they didn't bother either of us. Now when the bigots make comments, it's going to hurt, or piss one of us off—or both. It's not just in public, Ry. It's here, between us. You don't like my example of a woman on a date...but think about it. The roles are pretty well defined for you, sexually."

"What the—"

"I mean I'm *not* a woman...and yeah, I know how that sounds, but bear with me. I don't mean that women are lesser, but if you were taking one home for the night, you'd expect to get lucky, but I bet you've never wondered if you were going to take it up the ass..."

"Why do you keep trying to bring it down to only sex? I told you before if all we ever do is what we've already tried, I'm good with that."

It was hard to think with Cliff straddling Ryan's hips, dragging their bare, leaking cocks together. Ryan's breath left him on a whoosh as his heart thundered erratically. "Yeah, you said you're good with that...but what if I'm not? What if I want you right where you are right now? Under me? All that gorgeous tanned skin spread out like my own personal buffet?"

Cliff's eyes darkened and his tongue darted out to moisten his lips as he stared down at Ryan as if he was the best meal he'd never tasted—yet. A line from a childhood book popped into his head...*the better to eat you...* At this moment, Cliff looked like Ryan's own personal big bad, and he was fucking hungry.

"What if I want more...want to bury my face between your cheeks and rim you until you lose your mind? What if I want to stick my cock in deep and pound until my balls slap against your ass? What if I want to fuck you through this mattress?

"Because oh, yeah, Ryan, *baby*...if we do this...this whole couple thing...you can make bank on it. That's going to happen.

Ryan's ass clenched, setting off a series of tremors that raced through him at Cliff's words. They left him with only one possible response—

"Yes, please…"

Chapter Thirteen

Dropping his newfound insecurity was a lot easier thought about than actually done. Never one to suffer from lack of confidence, this situation with Ryan had Cliff more off-balance than he'd ever been in his life. For the first time he was seriously thinking about a long-term commitment and he was unsure if a relationship beyond the bedroom would have any lasting power once it hit the light of day.

Not that Cliff needed—or expected—any sort of PDA. It was hard to imagine himself ever walking down a street holding anyone's hand—but Ryan's? Just the idea had him wanting to shake his head. Ryan as a best friend meant someone he spent three or four nights a week hanging out with. Watching television, playing softball, going to ball games, you name it, they were usually doing it together. If this…relationship…was going to evolve, it had to go beyond fuck buddy status.

Ryan had said he loved him…and god knew he loved him back…but now Cliff knew a fear of losing what had barely just started.

Yes, please…

Cliff studied Ryan's face. Heavy lids couldn't disguise the gold flecks sparking in his hazel eyes, and Ryan's tongue slid over his sexy full lower lip. Ryan's face was nearly as familiar as his own, maybe more so. Because Cliff wasn't exactly the sort to stand around looking at himself in the mirror. How many hours had they sat across from each other, next to each other? He'd even had Ryan under him a time or two during pick-up football games on the base. But nothing could ever have prepared him for this change in their relationship.

"Please, Cliff," he repeated. "Show me…"

Unable to resist the plea, Cliff lunged forward to take the lips he'd been obsessed with since the moment he'd first tasted them. As soon as Ryan opened for him, Cliff shoved his tongue inside, tangling it with Ryan's in a kiss that was wet and hard and dirty.

Ryan gasped then pressed into the assault, his big eyes blinked rapidly then drifted closed. Smiling into the kiss, Cliff allowed himself one final thought about just how…odd it was to be kissing Ryan Matthews. A fierce possessiveness raced through him and then his only thought was how to make this good for Ryan. So good that he never looked at another—man or woman—again.

Slowly, Cliff lowered himself, stretching out until his body aligned with Ryan's, their hard lengths pressed together. As good as it would have felt to stay right there, chest to chest, thigh against thigh, cocks nestled together, Cliff continued a slow slide down his lover's body. Ryan's moans spurred him on as Cliff nipped and licked his way over the tight six-pack, following the dark blond trail until he found the treasure he sought.

A rough urgency drove at Cliff, until all he knew was a desire to claim. It was as impossible to say no to this burning hunger as it would have been to stop breathing. Ryan opened his legs, the right knee bent at an angle that exposed him. Cliff groaned at the sight, and clamped his hand on Ry's leg, guiding him to pull his leg farther onto his chest and hold it there.

With one hand on Ryan's leg, Cliff rested his elbow on the mattress and buried his face, breathing deeply of the already familiar scent. He angled his head to take one of Ryan's balls into his mouth. As he gently sucked on the sac of skin, Ryan moaned again, and a shiver raced through him. Cliff alternated between pulling on the tender flesh and swiping his tongue along the smooth skin behind Ry's balls. When Ryan's hips bucked and jerked, Cliff gripped his ass, encouraging him to roll up and give him more access.

The soft pucker of Ryan's ass called to him, begging to be taken. With a broad swipe of tongue, he began an assault on Ryan's pucker. He pulled the muscled cheeks apart, alternately jabbing his tongue and tapping his finger against the fleshy pucker. Cliff kept his hand on Ryan's leg, effectively holding him in place as he inserted the tip of a finger, then licked, slicking Ryan's ass, stretching the muscles. Finger, tongue, teeth, lips, again and again as the tight ring of muscles relaxed under his attention.

Ryan's hips pumped as Cliff blew gently over the now moist skin then flicked his tongue out to tease again.

"God—what the hell are you doing to me?" Ryan rasped out.

"Told you. Gonna make you lose your mind."

"Too late...want you now, Cliff. No more..."

Cliff pressed his lips to Ryan's tight sac and laughed darkly. "Not your call this time, baby..."

Taking the begging as a good sign, Cliff rose to his knees then added lube to the already spit-slick hole. He pressed in two fingers, working them slowly, letting his knuckles drag over the sensitive ring of muscles. He continued to slide in and out, tapping against Ryan's gland every few strokes. Cliff swirled his tongue over the head of his fat cock and lapped up the pre-cum as Ryan fell apart beneath him.

"Love sucking you…"

"Unnh…" Ryan grunted.

Feeling nearly as desperate as Rhino sounded, Cliff rose and reached for the lube once again. He poured a generous amount into his palm, stroking his own shaft, slapping it against Ryan's crease, spreading slick everywhere.

With the broad cap pressed to the tight muscle, Cliff rasped his hand over Ryan's shin, meeting his lover's gaze. "Nice and easy now, honey. Push back to relax your muscle," he said.

Ryan's lids closed briefly as Cliff breached his ass. Sweat dotted his forehead and cheeks, and his lips parted on a soft intake of breath. Cliff murmured some nonsense words as he rubbed his hands over Ry's legs.

"Look at me, Rhino…"

Ryan's heavy lids rose slowly, his eyes dark with passion when they met Cliff's.

"Ah, Cliff… Give me more…"

With full permission to move, Cliff pushed slowly in, withdrew, then sheathed himself in the hot channel once again. With every thrust of his hips, he picked up speed, his breath puffing like a steam engine.

Ryan chanted Cliff's name each time he bottomed out, his balls slapping against Ryan's body, and wondered which stroke would be his last. He was so close to coming, his balls were practically inside out. Yet as ready as his body was to reach completion, his mind…his heart begged for the moment to last. He'd never felt this way before—never had this connection. He couldn't find enough words—or maybe just the right words—to convey all the emotions, the feelings burning through him, setting his very soul on fire. He felt as though he were truly inside Ry in every way possible. Looking down at his lover—just thinking the word made him smile—he knew the enormity of the sensations Ryan was experiencing. Ry's face was like a living movie, showing every bit of lust, of need, of wanton desire. And something else—something more. Something Cliff had never dared dream he'd see, something he never believed he'd return so fully. *Love.*

Leaning down, Cliff's lips hovered over Ryan's mouth, their breath mingling as he gripped Ryan's cock and began to stroke in time with the rhythm of their mating.

"Can't hold on…" Ryan gasped. The words were barely out of his mouth when his ass clamped down on Cliff's cock. His hips stuttered as ropes of creamy white spurted from Ry, covering his hand and splattering on their stomachs.

Two more quick thrusts was all he could manage before his own orgasm lit him up from inside, sending a shower of lights behind his lids, and sending his heart into a free fall from twenty-thousand feet.

"Should have run when you had the chance, Rhino…"

Cliff stretched out over Ryan, who brought his legs up to tangle them with his, their bodies joined with the sticky proof of their mutual pleasure. The sudden tensing of the body beneath him was the only warning he got, then Ryan reared up to flip them back over. Landing on top of Cliff, Rhino took Cliff's mouth in a sensual kiss.

"No need to run, baby," Ryan said when he finally drew back.

Cliff blinked up at the familiar face in the unfamiliar position. "Is this just sex, Ryan? I know you said you love me, but…tell me you're feeling the same things I am. Tell me this scares you as much as it does me…"

"It doesn't scare me, baby. Not anymore." He paused, as if carefully choosing his words. "It did at first. When Ty told me he thought I had feelings for you that were more than what friends usually feel for each other…I thought maybe his head injury was working against him. Because the one thing I was certain of—I wasn't gay. Or at least I really did enjoy women. I mean that's a thing a nearly forty-year-old man ought to know about himself. But bisexual? Somehow that freed me to really consider the suggestion. I knew I needed to do some serious soul-searching."

Ryan nuzzled into Cliff's neck, breathing deeply before drawing his lobe between his teeth and biting softly.

Cliff sighed when Ryan released him. Raising his face, Ryan closed his eyes and remained silent for a moment while a small smile played over his lips.

What memories were playing in Ryan's mind? Cliff had obviously been Ryan's first BJ...first fuck... Would he forever be haunted by his decision to drive past SEAL Beach without stopping to see Ryan? Cliff had honestly believed he'd been acting in Ryan's best interest, but he should have known his best friend wouldn't accept defeat.

Cliff wanted to growl at the unwelcome vision of Ryan visiting a gay club or going out with another man to test Ty's theory—someone who wasn't Cliff. It was the same sort of thing Rhino'd done years ago when he'd decided he liked redheads. They'd gone to every on-base club and a couple of off-base ones as well, so Rhino could search for gingers. Not an easy task, since they'd been in Yokosuka, Japan, at the time, and black had been the predominant hair color.

"Tell me you didn't make a test run while I was..." he begged, his voice harsh. While his brain acknowledged the standard operating procedure for training before any mission, the fault lines in his heart prepared to shatter with the unwelcome news.

"While you were being an ass?" Ryan supplied. "Oh, but I did test things out." Ryan grinned. Something in Cliff's face must have warned him he'd gone too far, because the smile faded and he reached up to cup Cliff's face in both hands. "Not that kind of test, baby. I told you I watched porn...and well...there might be a few new toys in the bedside drawer at home.

"There's only been you. You think I need more proof that this is what I want? Baby, you're the baddest ass I know. Cool Hand, right? I've watched you dismantle a bomb that would have taken out half a city block. Why does this scare you?"

Cliff dragged his hands along Rhino's flanks, over his ass, then back up his spine while the words fought their way out.

"I've never wanted anything in my life as much as I want you. This. Us."

Suddenly, Cliff couldn't seem to shut his mouth. "I've spent the better part of twenty years looking at you, but never seeing you...never seeing the possibility of what we could have. You're giving up everything...every-fucking-thing for me? I don't know what to do with that—I'm not certain it's something I deserve, but I know I don't want it to end. I don't want us to end."

Ryan captured his words in a kiss that spun out and had Cliff's cock twitching with renewed interest. He bit Cliff's lower lip when he drew back and their gazes locked.

"This right here?" Ryan said, his thumbs stroking over Cliff's jawline. "I want you this close. I want to look at you every day...every night...and know that you're mine. You matter. This matters."

Chapter Fourteen

Standing on legs that still shook slightly from the intensity of his second orgasm of the morning, Ryan finished soaping his body, and hoped like hell Cliff was making coffee. After the early morning drive from San Diego and then making love with Cliff—both bottom and top, thank you very much—he might just need a ten-hour nap.

Lifting his balls to rinse away the soap, Ryan winced. Damn. If he was sore, how would Cliff's ass be feeling after the pounding it had just taken? He'd wager horse riding was off the day's things-to-do list.

There were a lot of ways to make love, and they would try them all in time, but damn…lying on his back and pushing up into the hot silken heat of Cliff's ass was a new personal favorite memory. Especially once Cliff's hips began to roll in a front to back pattern that deepened Ryan's stroke. It gave him a whole new appreciation for twerking.

A knock on the door signaled Cliff's arrival, and Ryan quickly finished rinsing.

"Hey, did you drown in here?" Cliff asked over the pounding of the water. "I've got your coffee…"

"See? I knew I loved you for a reason…" Ryan said as he shut off the water.

Grabbing a thick white towel from the bar next to the shower, he stepped out of the stall and rubbed the water from his face and head. He'd intended to dry quickly, but slowed once he caught Cliff following every movement of his hands as he dragged the towel across his body.

"Dayum, Snides. You look hungry…"

The chirp of Ryan's phone from the other room saved him from having to admit his cock might need a little more recovery time—

Wrapping the towel around his waist, he moved to the bedroom and snatched his phone from the nightstand.

"Matthews," he said when he answered.

"You don't call, you don't write…"

"Hey, Draco," he said, flopping back onto the mattress and accepting the cup of coffee Cliff offered. Their gazes lingered for a moment as Ryan switched the phone to speaker and set it on the nightstand. "Sorry about that, I've been busy with my retirement processing."

"Are you clear on the shooting?" Draco asked.

"You really are out of the loop. Cliff's clear on the shooting. *I* wasn't there…remember? Cliff says thanks for the lawyer by the way."

"Cliff can speak for himself, Rhino," Cliff growled, lowering his brows in Ryan's direction. "And yes, thanks again, Draco. The cops were cool, but Jefferson was just the right kind of smart to get the prosecutor to back down."

"Getting you a lawyer was the least I could do, believe me. Retirement processing, Rhino? You're turning down Six? Are you sure this is the right time? Don't make the same mistake I did and get out before you're ready…"

Ryan laughed. "Trust me, I'm sure. Besides we all know it was only the *opportunity* to try for Six that I turned down…there was no guarantee I'd actually make the cut. I'm completely comfortable with my decision."

"Good. Glad to hear it."

Ryan laughed. "Nice about-face."

"Meh, I didn't want to influence your decision. If you're happy with your decision, then I'm happy for you. Which makes this conversation easier…"

"Oh, was this supposed to be difficult?" Ryan asked. He took a quick sip of coffee, careful to not burn his tongue—just in case he needed it later.

"What conversation?" Cliff asked. "Is everything okay, Draco?"

The man's heavy sigh carried clearly over the phone. "Have you thought any more about staying on the third floor, Cliff?"

Ryan's brows rose as he looked at Cliff. What was this? Had he and Draco made some plans while he'd been keeping Ryan at arm's length?

Cliff's mouth pressed into a tight straight line for an instant, then he shook his head slightly, as if Draco could see him. He stepped over to the bed and sat next to Ryan before answering. "I appreciate the offer, Draco, but like I told you before, I'm not sure I'm going back to San Diego—"

"What?" Ryan asked, his tone sharp and his stomach tightening around the coffee he'd swallowed.

"Why's that, Snides?" Draco asked.

It was Cliff's turn to sigh. "I wasn't sure I'd want to go back after what happened—besides, I still don't know what I'm going to do."

"We're," Ryan snapped. "What *we're* going to do."

There was a pause as Ryan glared at Cliff, and they both forgot about Draco as they dove into a very private conversation.

"Okay. What *we're* going to do," Cliff amended. "We've been focused on our careers for so long...we should at least acknowledge the possibility exists this thing between us is a substitute—"

"Cliff, stop overanalyzing—"

"It's not that. I want to give you a way out, Ryan. Entrance and egress. Six months from now—"

"I'll still love you."

Cliff closed his eyes for a moment, as if he were savoring the words.

"I want to believe you, Ry, really I do." The normally pale blue-gray of his eyes shifted to storm clouds. "But, Ryan, you've got your own coming out to do...people you've known for years will know. And for me—that whole situation at the club—"

Draco cleared his throat, reminding them they'd been in the middle of a different conversation.

"I see you two have a few things to talk about, but I've got something to say about that. Yeah, Cliff, you might have fucked up by getting caught in that situation at the club. You paid a price. Think you're the first person that's happened to? Walk down Main Street, USA. Which person there knows or cares what you did in that one hour of your life? Or in the thousands of hours that came before that minute you let yourself get cuffed to a bed.

"You want to go to Coronado—to the base? Then hell yes, someone you bump into might know. So the fuck what? Nobody really cares. San Diego is a big enough city and has been your home for a lot of years."

"So why'd you call, Draco?" Ryan asked, suddenly anxious to talk with Cliff in private to make sure he didn't sink back into his thoughts.

"I have a proposition for you and Cliff. This isn't something easily explained over the phone—especially since I'm expecting my daily interrogation with Kam in a few minutes. You'd think his injuries would have slowed him down. Under other circumstances, I might find him rather...attractive."

Ryan laughed. "Uh huh. Okay, Cliff and I will come visit but we're out of town. I'm not sure when we're heading back—we have a few decisions to make about what's next—"

"Yeah, it's about that. Rhino...despite the two dead men who came back to finish things, I'm not sure that everything's—" Draco blew out a breath. "I think I'd like some protection. I'd like to hire the two of you, so come see me before you make any decisions."

"Oh...uh...sure. We can talk about it, but I don't think—"

"Rhino," Draco's voice was a harsh whisper over the line. "I'm going out of here in a chair. I need—"

Cliff's gaze met his, and in that moment, he knew they were on the same page. There might still be plenty of questions to answer about their future, but for now, their path was clear.

"Say no more, Draco. Cliff and I will be there tonight."

~~The End~~

Also Available

Deuce Coop

For nearly five years, Deuce managed to keep his gang out of serious trouble, but a favor for a friend of a friend puts Deuce in a hell of a spot—take temporary—and unwilling—custody of a young man in a relationship that's way over his head or leave him in the path of a near-certain death? Despite his decision to leave college-boy's safety to chance in order to protect his gang from potential kidnapping charges, Cooper ends up cuffed to Deuce's bed and he discovers fate has a different solution in mind.

When Cooper McElroy is kidnapped by bikers, he has no idea his life is about to change forever. From the moment he meets their sinfully sexy leader Deuce, he realizes the attraction might be more dangerous than the situation the bikers claim to have saved him from. Kept in an isolated location, Cooper discovers this is one gang that doesn't seem to have issues with territory—it's all share and share alike. Cooper's only protection is Deuce's order declaring him strictly off limits. But the more time Cooper spends with Deuce, the more his body insists it knows what it wants—so who's going to save him now?

Cooper's about to discover a new life on the open road...and what it means to be part of a gang that shares almost everything. Will he continue to seek his freedom or beg the gang to take him on the ride of his life?

Episode I

In this episode, Cooper receives a most unpleasant surprise from his boyfriend, who refuses to take no for an answer. When a stranger intervenes, Cooper finds himself on the back of the stranger's bike and wonders if he's just been pulled from the frying pan only to be tossed straight into the fire.

Don't miss the other installments of Deuce Coop: Taken (Episode 1), Deadlocked (Episode 2), Collision (Episode 3), Dark Desires (Episode 4) Repercussions (Episode 5) and Truth and Consequences (Episode 6)

About the Author

Laura lives on waterfront property in Arizona because she's always wanted to be an oxymoron. She once enjoyed hobbies such as gardening and travel—now the characters in her head compel her to tell their stories, so she writes. (It doesn't actually help quiet the voices—but it keeps the folks in the white jackets at bay.)

She shares her home with an ever-revolving cast of characters—some of whom are actually real—and is living her dream of building her own version of the Willow Springs Ranch.

With over fifty published novels and novellas, Laura is an international bestselling author of erotic romances, romantic suspense, urban fantasy, and Highland romances. Her books can be found at all major online retailers.

Connect with her online:
Twitter: http://twitter.com/lauraharner
Facebook: http://facebook.com/lauraharner

For my blog, book news, and to read free excerpts visit:

http://lauraharner.com